"An exciting, original and suspense-laden who-dunit…A simply fabulous mystery starring a likeable, dedicated heroine…"

—*Midwest Book Review*

"A delightful protagonist…a well-crafted mystery."

—*Romantic Times*

"There can't be too many golden retrievers in mystery fiction for my taste."

—*Deadly Pleasures*

"An intriguing heroine, a twisty tale, a riveting finale, and a golden retriever to die for. [This book] will delight mystery fans and enchant dog lovers."

—*Carolyn Hart*

"Has everything—wonderful characters, surprising twists, great dialogue. Donna Ball knows dogs, knows the Smoky Mountains, and knows how to write a page turner. I loved it."

—*Beverly Connor*

"Very entertaining…combines a likeable heroine and a fascinating mystery…a story of suspense with humor and tenderness."

—*Carlene Thompson*

## THE RAINE STOCKTON DOG MYSTERY SERIES BOOKS IN ORDER:

# HOME OF THE BRAVE

www.donnaball.net

Published by Blue Merle Publishing
Drawer H
Mountain City, Georgia 30562
www.bluemerlepublishing.com

ISBN 13: 9780985774875
ISBN 10: 0985774878
First printing September 2014

This is a work of fiction. All places, characters, events and organizations mentioned in this book are either the product of the
author's imagination, or used fictitiously.

Cover art by www.bigstock.com

# HOME OF THE BRAVE

## A RAINE STOCKTON DOG MYSTERY BOOK #9

Donna Ball

# CHAPTER ONE

It was twelve forty-five on a Thursday afternoon and pouring down rain when I glanced in my rearview mirror and saw the flashing blue lights. Automatically I tapped the brakes in acknowledgement and received a blast of the siren in return. Everyone in the Hanover County Sheriff's Department knew my car and this was the way we customarily greeted each other. I edged over to the curb so that he could pass, but didn't slow down much. I was in a hurry. When the car didn't try to pull around me, I resumed my lane and kept going. I might even have increased my speed a little.

I was closing Dog Daze Boarding and Training early for the weekend and I had six dogs checking out between two and three. Furthermore, I had promised my young friend Melanie I'd be ready to leave by three thirty sharp and she was so excited about our big weekend together that she had already called me three times that morning to make sure I was on schedule. The truth was, I was not. I always seemed to be running behind these days.

1

I had never gotten a speeding ticket in Hanover County in my life, mostly because I was a good driver, but also because I knew the traffic officers would usually give you an extra eight or ten miles per hour over the speed limit outside the city limits and away from school zones. The county was just too big, and the highways too open, to enforce a forty-five-miles-per-hour speed limit consistently. Usually I took every bit of that extra ten miles per hour, and today was no exception.

That was why I was so surprised when my ears were pierced by the repeated wail of a siren. The blue lights strobed so close on my bumper that they actually hurt my eyes. I said out loud, "What the...?" and stared at the mirror. My back windshield was a sheet of rain and I couldn't see anything but the racing blue lights. I pulled over, impatient and annoyed as I tried to recall who was on patrol duty on Thursdays and would think it was cute to try to harass me in the pouring rain.

I waited and watched the mirrors but saw nothing but flashing lights reflected in the rain. I waited so long that I almost ran out of patience and started the car again. Finally there was movement. I watched in my rear mirror as a tall figure in a glistening rain slicker and plastic-covered cap slowly approached my door. I rolled my eyes impatiently and stabbed the button that lowered the window. Rain water splashed in and I shouted, "For heaven's sake, Deke, is that you? Are you crazy? I'm in a hurry!" By this time my face was splattered with water, the hand and arm nearest the window were soaked, and rain was blowing in on my upholstery. I closed the window and watched him continue his cautious approach through the mirror.

Only it wasn't a him. The person who eventually leaned down to peer through my window into the car was female, African American and grim-faced. And there was no such person on staff of the Hanover County Sheriff's Department. She was not wearing the uniform of a state trooper or anyone else with the authority to pull me over on a deserted highway. Automatically, I reached for my phone.

She rapped sharply on my window with her knuckles. "Roll down your window, ma'am," she commanded.

I did so, mostly because I wanted a better look at her. But when my hand moved toward the button, she stepped back from the car door and I couldn't see much of anything except the way her hands remained close to her utility belt—just in case, I suppose, I tried to make a break for it.

The sound of pelting rain was thunderous, so I had to shout to be heard over it. "Who are you?"

She approached the car again and leaned down to look at me. She had gorgeous ebony skin, now glistening with rain water, and a collar-length braid of coarse black hair. She wore no makeup, but she didn't need any. What she did wear, to my astonishment, was a Hanover County Sheriff's Department deputy badge on the outside of her slicker.

She said, "License and registration, please."

I peered at her through the rain. "You're new, right?"

She repeated, "License and registration."

I pulled out my wallet and produced my driver's license, mostly because I didn't know what else to do. My vehicle registration was in the glove compartment. "Listen," I said, handing her my license, "I know you don't know who I am…"

She glanced at my driver's license, and then at me. Rain bounced off her cap, making a sound like tiny pellets of gravel as it hit the plastic. "It says here your name is Raine Stockton. I need to see your registration."

I sighed and unfastened my seatbelt. "I'm sorry I was speeding, but I guess they didn't tell you the limit isn't very strictly enforced on this part of the highway." I stretched across the seat and punched the button that released the glove compartment door. "Maybe you could just give me a warning, and check with the office later."

The glove compartment door fell open and the small interior light illuminated the contents. I started to reach inside but she said sharply, "Move your hands away from the glove compartment, ma'am."

I scowled in annoyance and confusion, and then I saw what had caught her attention. I groaned out loud and sat back.

She said, "Place your hands on the wheel."

I did.

"Do you have a license to carry a concealed weapon?"

I am a dog trainer by trade, a volunteer search and rescue worker by vocation. A certain amount of that work has, over the years, been done at the behest of the sheriff's department, and after one or two close calls, my ex-husband—who wasn't my ex then—persuaded me to start including a handgun in the emergency supplies I kept in my pack. He had a point. These mountains are thick with timber rattlers and copperheads, not to mention the occasional mountain lion, and I have not only myself but my dog to protect. When I return from a hike, I usually put the gun in the glove compartment of my car, which is always locked, until I remember to take it inside and put it back in the gun safe.

I hadn't remembered to do that yet.

I sighed. "Of course I do. It's in the glove compartment with the gun. And my vehicle registration." I did not, of course, reach for it. She might be a rookie, but I knew the procedure. My father was a judge, my uncle a sheriff, and I had been married to a law officer for most of my adult life. That would be the same ex-husband who had persuaded me to get a license-to-carry in the first place. The irony was not lost on me.

She took a step back from the door. "Please step outside."

I looked at the rain, looked at her, and replied, "I don't think so." I had just come from the Labelle's Hair and Nails, where I'd paid eighty-five dollars to have my shoulder-length brunette curls trimmed and highlighted into a cute, above-the-ears cut that I was wild about. It's not that I'm particularly vain, and the real reason behind the haircut was that the long hair had gotten to be completely unmanageable around the dogs. But there was someone I wanted to show off to before the new style was ruined. Besides, it was eighty-five dollars. I picked up my phone.

She said sharply, "Ma'am, put down the phone."

"Hold on."

"Please put down the phone and step outside."

I glanced up at her incredulously. "In this rain? Seriously? Just give me a minute and we'll have this straightened out."

I was just about to push Send when my car door suddenly flew open and a strong hand grabbed my arm, pulling me from the car. My phone landed on the front seat, far out of reach. I gave a cry of protest and instinctively wrestled against her grip. She grabbed both of my arms, hard, behind my back, and pushed me up against the car. She was really strong. I cried, "Hey!" and when I did she seemed to realize she might have overreacted. She eased her grip, just a little, but I couldn't have escaped if I'd wanted to as she turned me around and marched me through the rain back toward the flashing blue lights.

I probably should have been frightened, and I was, a little. But mostly I was shocked, and embarrassed, and only my very good sense kept me from trying to wrench away, or at least to give her a piece of my mind. That kind of behavior hardly ever worked out well for the perpetrator, but I think I understood for the first time why so many people instinctively fought back when an officer made an arrest. When confronted with violence, you tend to react with violence, and before you know it everything is out of hand. As far as I was concerned things were already out of hand, but fortunately for this bully, whoever she was, I was a model of self-control. That did not mean I wouldn't have a thing or two to say about the situation as soon as she let me go.

I wasn't wearing a raincoat, and my shorts and tee shirt were quickly soaked. My hair dripped rainwater into my eyes. My sneakers squished as I splashed through the small river of puddles that had accumulated along the side of the road, and none of this did anything to improve my temper. We got these brief intense showers just about every afternoon in the summer here in the mountains and you'd think I would be more prepared. I wasn't. And that, as was about to become obvious, wasn't even the biggest mistake I made that day.

The vehicle parked behind mine with the flash bar on top was a sleek black SUV, and I felt my first real prickle of alarm because the Hanover County Sheriff's Department did not own a black SUV. Then I saw the unmistakable HCSD logo lettered on the door in white, and I was even more confused because beneath that familiar logo in large white letters was written K-9 Unit. I blinked and stared, my growing anger overcome by curiosity. Since when did we have a K-9 unit?

I twisted around to look at my captor. "Who are you?" I asked for the second time.

Her only reply was a brusque, "Wait in the unit."

She opened the back door of the vehicle and guided me inside without another word. I had no way of knowing whether she was placing me under arrest or simply getting me out of the rain, but at this point I was far less interested in the answer to that question than I was in the K-9 Unit stenciled on the side of the car. The cold air from the air-conditioning vents prickled my wet skin and the smell of car leather and gun oil were mixed with the familiar, welcoming scent of wet dog fur. As soon as I was in the backseat, she closed the door and I heard the twin locks snap. I barely noticed her departure, however, because I was completely captivated by the magnificent canine creature in the front seat, separated from me only by a security grid.

Even in these dire circumstances, I couldn't help smiling at him, and I almost forgot to be angry. I've never met a dog who didn't make me smile, and besides, my problems weren't his fault. He looked like a German shepherd, an easy mistake for most people to make. His short, thick coat was a golden tan and his muzzle and ears distinctively marked with black. He had keen, intelligent brown eyes that turned to look at me assessingly through the bars. He was a Belgian Malinois, one of the most impressive breeds in the world for police and military work. How in the world could our little town afford something like this? And why hadn't anyone told me?

I am a dog lover by nature, which might be obvious from the kind of work I do—most of which is with my golden retriever, Cisco, who, while he might be a little short on blue ribbons, has saved enough lives to become pretty famous around here. I'm also trial secretary of our local agility club, vice president of the tracking club, and am the entire population of the local chapter of the Golden Retriever Rescue and Purebred Rescue, as well as an active volunteer with the humane society. There is absolutely no chance of my being uncomfortable in any situation in which dogs are present. This was no exception.

I said softly, "Hello there, big fellow." I believe in talking to dogs. Most of the time they're more interesting than people, and this one already had a huge advantage over his handler, being the only one of the team who was not trying to put me in jail. I added, "Welcome to the force. Nice to meet you. Really."

He regarded me coolly for another moment, seemed to decide I was no immediate threat, and turned his attention back to the direction in which his handler had gone. I relaxed and settled back against the seat. Things were definitely looking up, now that there was a dog involved.

Or at least that's what I thought.

Less than five minutes later the front door opened and the woman got behind the wheel of the car. She had my papers, now limp with rain, in her hand, along with my pistol. She said, glancing at me in the mirror, "Miss Stockton, are you aware that your license to carry a concealed weapon has expired?"

*Oh, crap.* The smug sarcasm with which I had been about to greet her vanished like sun behind a cloud. "That's just great," I muttered. Then, because she seemed to be waiting for an answer, I added irritably, "Of course I didn't know! Listen, if you'll just radio the office and tell them what happened…"

She said, "It's against the law to carry a concealed weapon in the state of North Carolina without a permit. I'm going to have to take you in."

I sat forward abruptly. "*What?*"

The dog swiveled his head at me and gave a soft growl of warning. I didn't blame him. He was just doing his job.

I sat back, but my annoyance was only growing. I was cold, wet and late, and my usual good nature—which was better on some days than others—was fast disintegrating. "You know they have a name for overzealous cops around here, don't you? It's called the Barney Fife Syndrome, and I never saw a more perfect example of it. This is definitely not the way to settle in to a new community, I'll tell you that much. You have no idea how sorry you're about to be, but don't say I didn't try to warn you. Aren't you supposed to read me my rights or something? "

She put the car in gear without response.

"Hey!" I twisted around to look at my car, sitting forlornly by the side of the road. "Hey, what about my car? Did you at least lock it? I've got stuff inside!"

She pulled out onto the road without response, and I flung my head back against the seat in a rather childish display of exasperation. Needless to say, I made no further attempts at conversation. Neither she nor her dog looked at me again.

# Chapter Two

By the time we parked in front of the Public Safety building the rain had stopped, the sun was out, and the steam that rose from the wet pavement reminded me of the slow burn my temper was doing. She opened the door and I got out, and this time when she took my arm I snapped, "I know the way."

She released my arm, and I gave a self-satisfied toss of my wet, ruined hair. But before I could get too carried away with self-congratulations, she spoke a single guttural command in German, and the Malinois appeared out of nowhere to stand at my side. I couldn't help being impressed. With the dog on one side of me and the officer on the other, I was escorted into the building. Even if I had been a real criminal, there was absolutely no way I would have tried anything under those circumstances. *Now that*, I thought, sliding an admiring glance down at the dog, *is what I call teamwork.*

But as soon as we crossed the threshold of the sheriff's department and I saw the surprise on the receptionist's face, my annoyance was back.

"Hey, Raine," she said, trying to cover her confusion. "Cute haircut."

"Thanks."

Then she looked concerned. "Are you okay?"

I said, probably ungraciously, "I'm soaking wet. Do you have a towel?"

She actually stood to search for one, but the officer handed her an envelope with my paperwork in it, and she sank back to her chair again. The woman jerked her head curtly toward a row of chairs that were lined up against the wall. "Wait there," she said.

I rolled my eyes and walked over to one of the chairs, wet shoes squishing. When I sat down, she gave the dog another curt command in German, and he positioned himself squarely in front of me, his intense, alert gaze watching me. I muttered, "Okay, now you're just showing off," as she walked over to one of the cubicles that the deputies used to fill out paperwork and make phone calls. I said to the receptionist, "Annabelle, what's the deal with…"

But Annabelle was on the phone and held up a finger for patience. I couldn't hear what she was saying, but I hoped it was about getting me out of there because patience was something that was in short supply for me at the moment.

There followed three or four of the most unpleasant moments I have ever spent around a dog, and this from a woman who spends most of her day picking up dog poop. A couple of deputies peeked over the top of their cubicles and grinned. One of the courthouse clerks stopped by to leave an envelope at the desk, did a double take when he saw me, and said, "Hey, Raine."

I said "Hey" back, and he left without asking any questions. Not that there was anything unusual about seeing me in the waiting area of the sheriff's department with a dog at my feet. I'm sure it was just the fact that I was soaking wet.

Annabelle put down the phone and gave me a smile that tried very hard not to look nervous. I remembered she had never been that comfortable around big dogs. She said, "It'll be just a few minutes."

I wasn't sure what would be just a few minutes, but before I could ask, she added pleasantly, "Big weekend planned?"

I decided to play along, mostly to demonstrate that I was completely unfazed by this absurd turn of events, but also because at the moment I couldn't see that I had much choice. "I'm going to be teaching at Camp Bowser Wowser." I kept my voice conversational, but loud enough so that Deputy Diligence, or whatever her name was, would have no trouble hearing just how unfazed I was. "It starts tomorrow, but the instructors are supposed to be there this afternoon, so…"

Her pale eyebrows shot up into her sandy, straight-cut bangs. "Bowsie Wowsie? What's that?"

"Bowser Wowser," I corrected. "It's a really cool camp for nine- to twelve-year-olds and their dogs. Usually they hold it over in Tennessee, but this year it's at the old Camp Bluebird, just off Highway 511."

"No kidding? I thought that place had shut down years ago. I was a counselor there as a kid."

"Me, too." Most of the people who grew up in this county had worked there during the summer at one time or another. It was one of the few ways for a teenager to make spending money—legally, that is. "I guess they haven't had any regular groups up there in a while, but it must still be in good enough shape to rent out for the weekend. The woman who runs the camp is pretty particular about the safety of the dogs. And kids, of course."

She smiled reminiscently. "Gosh, I had some good times there."

We chatted like that for another couple of minutes, each of us trying to ignore the fact that I was being held in custody by a guard dog that had been trained to kill. When the phone rang she snatched it up immediately, listened for a few minutes, and looked enormously relieved when she returned her attention to me.

"Buck said you should wait in his office, Raine," she said. "He's on his way."

"Great." I tilted my head toward my canine guard. "What about…?"

"Oh. Umm…"

But even as she looked around in some uneasiness, the dog's handler reemerged from her cubicle. She did not look in the least perturbed, although she surely had been informed of her gaffe by now. She said, "Nike, here!" And the big dog glided to her side—in a perfect obedience heel position, I might add.

Even though there was certainly no love lost on my part for his owner, anyone would have to be impressed by a dog who speaks two languages and executes positions so precise that he might have plotted them with a slide rule. It was easy to forget that very dog had held me hostage only moments ago, and with such dedicated intensity that I have no doubt that if I'd tried to move I'd now be on my way to the ER.

The officer said, "This way, please."

I just stared at her. "Really?" I gave a short shake of my head that scattered droplets of water across my shoulders and turned to make my way down the hall. "Nice dog, though," I added over my shoulder.

She might have pulled a gun on me, or set her dog on me at the very least, if Lyle Reston, one of Buck's deputies, hadn't fallen in step beside me at that moment. I'd gone to school with his older brother. "I'm heading that way, Deputy Smith," he said. "I've got this."

Well, at least she had a name, or part of one anyway. I didn't even bother to wait until we were out of earshot to ask, "Who *is* that?"

He smothered a grin. "Piece of work, isn't she? That's Deputy Sheriff Jolene Smith, and her partner Deputy Nike. A gift from Homeland Security. They just arrived Monday. The dog is fitting in just fine." He frowned a little. "Weird name, though. Who names their dog after a running shoe?"

I privately wondered the same thing, but was far more curious about the dog's origins than his name. I said, "Homeland Security, huh? Wow."

"The sheriff wants us to make her feel at home." His expression grew rueful as he paused outside the door to Buck's office. "I guess some of the boys have their own ideas about how to do that. Sorry you got wet. Do you want me to bring you some paper towels from the men's room?"

I looked at him suspiciously. "No. What do you mean, the boys have their own ideas?"

"Just don't be too mad." He opened the door to the office for me.

"I'm already mad," I told him, "and I'm running late. Who's going to take me back to my car?"

"I'll tell the sheriff you're waiting," Lyle said, and he left quickly as I stepped into the room, closing the door behind him.

The office hadn't changed much since my uncle had occupied it. It was a small, cluttered, olive drab space that smelled like burned coffee and hard-working men. There was a map of the county with magnetic pins, a bulletin board cluttered with memos and sticky notes, an oak desk scattered with folders and stacks of papers. The one window was cloudy with grime, which was just as well because the only view was that of the back parking lot. No wonder Buck preferred to spend his time elsewhere. Come to think of it, so had Uncle Roe.

My aunt and uncle were currently on vacation on the dog-friendly beaches of Topsail Island with their collie, Majesty (who was actually my collie, but they loved her so much I didn't make a point of it) and my cousins. They had all rented a beach house together for the next two weeks, and had invited me to join them as a matter of routine. Now I almost wished I had. And I really would love to know what my Uncle Roe would make of these new developments in the sheriff's department that he had run so efficiently for thirty years.

I glanced at my watch, frowned in annoyance, and briefly thought about leaving Buck a note and just walking out. Then something caught my eye on his desk—a half-unwrapped stack of eight-by-ten posters that looked as though they had just come from the printer. Curiously, I walked to the desk and picked one up. The face of a handsome man with wavy hair and good, honest eyes looked back at me; the face of a man I once had loved enough to marry, and had called my best friend since I was eight years old; the face of the man who had betrayed me in a way only someone you trust implicitly can do. It was the face of Acting Sheriff Buck Lawson, and beneath the black and white image was printed in bold black letters: VOTE CECIL "BUCK" LAWSON FOR SHERIFF NOVEMBER 6. And in a slightly smaller, italic font, *Justice...Integrity.*

I grunted softly with surprise and reexamined the poster. Buck had been appointed sheriff when my uncle retired unexpectedly last fall after a heart attack. I knew that if he wanted to keep the job he would have to be duly elected when the term of appointment expired, but no one had mentioned to me that he had actually decided to run. Of course, I had been a little busy keeping up with my own stuff, but still, you'd think someone would have mentioned it. Local election campaigns always started midsummer. I was beginning to feel a little out of touch.

The door opened and Buck came in. He had a way of entering a room, all shoulders and long strides, that always turned heads. My head was no exception. He came behind the desk, took the poster out of my hand and thrust another official-looking form at me in its place. He looked stern. "Fill out the application, pay your fee, and you'll get your gun back." He looked at me more closely and added, surprised, "You cut your hair."

I scowled first at him, and then at the paper. "It cost me eighty-five dollars."

"It would've been cheaper to get your permit renewed."

I turned the scowl back on him, more intensely. "That's it? No apology?"

"Speeding, resisting arrest, threatening an officer, carrying a concealed weapon... You're lucky you're not being strip-searched this minute."

My temper flared. "Come on, Buck! Are you freaking kidding me? Resisting arrest? How stupid do you think I am? She dragged me out of my car in the rain!"

"You know damn well you're supposed to inform an officer you're carrying when you're pulled over," he returned, glaring at me. "You're the daughter of a judge, for God's sake!"

I pushed on angrily, "And I never threatened anybody!" Of course, by then I did have a vague recollection of saying words like "I'm warning you" and "you'll be sorry," but I was in too deep to back off now. "I'll tell you what this office needs, and that's a training program on how to interact with the public! And if you want to know who's lucky, it's *you* that it was me she treated like that, because if it had been anybody else…" I was beginning to realize that I might not be making as much sense as I might have liked, so I concluded with a terse, "You know what I mean. What's the story with that girl? Does she really work here? How'd you get a K-9 unit, anyway? And how dare she arrest me!"

He blew out a breath and sat down in the sagging vinyl chair, pushing it back from the desk on squeaky wheels so that he could stretch out his long legs. He regarded me levelly across the sloppy stacks of file folders and unanswered phone message slips. "Her name is Jolene Smith and if you try calling her a 'girl' to her face she'll probably punch your lights out. The county got a grant through some kind of Homeland Security program and she was assigned here. She was a K-9 handler in the military. Nike is a specialist in explosives detection."

I couldn't hide my skepticism. "A bomb-sniffing dog? Here? Well, that explains why you put her on highway patrol."

"Come on, Raine, cut me some slack." He looked mildly uncomfortable. "We're figuring it out as we go, here. Besides, she's got to learn the territory somehow."

"She wouldn't even let me make a phone call! She never once told me her name or showed me her badge or read me my rights!"

"That's because you were never under arrest."

"I told her to call you! She didn't even run my tag!"

He pushed his fingers through his hair, lips tightening briefly. "Actually, she did," he admitted. His expression grew rueful. "Look, Raine, you know how it is with a new man on the force. It looks like a couple of the boys thought Jo was due for a little hazing and you happened to be in the right place at the wrong time."

I couldn't help noticing that he seemed to be wasting no time with formalities. She had only been here three days and already she was "Jo."

"It seems Deke and Mike spotted your car on Turnbull Road and called in a possible sighting of a stolen vehicle... You know Jessie Connor, right? He reported his car stolen yesterday morning, and he drives a green Explorer, like yours."

"Half the people in this county drive green Explorers!"

He ignored me. "I guess they thought it would be a good joke on her if she pulled you over and accused you of driving a stolen vehicle."

"That's stupid!"

"Damn stupid is what it was," he countered sharply with a frown. "If I didn't need a full complement for the holiday weekend, I'd suspend them both without pay."

Monday was the Fourth of July, and the population of our little mountain paradise would easily double this weekend with tourists, hikers, boaters and vacation home owners. Restaurants and retail shops would prosper; so would traffic jams, pickpockets and bar fights. This was the beginning of the official high season in the Smokey Mountains, and from now until November everyone would be operating at full capacity, including the sheriff's office.

He let the frown go in a way that was typically Buck, and went on, "Anyway, Jo ran your tag when she pulled you over, and she also called the office for a background check..."

I smothered another exclamation of outrage but he held up a hand for forbearance. "And I'm guessing that's when she figured out she'd been set up."

"*She*'d been set up?"

"But instead of taking a joke, she decided to play it straight. After all, you *were* speeding. The expired permit was just good luck."

I stared at him belligerently. "For whom?"

He lifted one shoulder in a shrug. "She wanted to make a point. Don't worry, the guys have got one hell of a reaming-out coming. It won't happen again."

I waited. "And her? Aren't you going to talk to her?"

"We're lucky to have her, Raine. A little place like this with a $50,000 K-9 team? Not a boat I want to rock. And you should see that dog work." His eyes sparked with admiration as he spoke. The love of dogs—or at least one dog—was still the one thing we had in common.

I said shortly, "I have no problem with her dog." Then I added seriously, "Buck, you might not be as lucky as you think. Most people are afraid of police dogs, and this is a small town. A lot of folks are going to think that $50,000 could have been spent in better ways."

He gave an impatient shake of his head. "It doesn't work like that. We had to spend it on the K-9 team or lose it. That was the whole point."

"I'm just saying, it's not like you need one to break up street gangs or sniff out bombs at the courthouse, especially since we only have court twice a month. And I don't care what you say, your girl there is never going to win Miss Congeniality. If she goes around treating everybody like she did me today, your expensive K-9 team can end up being one giant liability." I looked meaningfully at the stack of election posters on his desk. "I'd think about it, if I were you."

He looked at me thoughtfully for a moment. "You might be right. We probably need some kind of public awareness campaign. Get a story in the paper, send her around to the schools..."

"School is out," I reminded him.

"Say," he said suddenly, "are you and Cisco going to that dog camp this weekend?"

I was uneasy. "How did you know about that?"

"They had to get their permit from me. I don't suppose you could…"

"In the first place, no," I retorted, "and in the second place, are you crazy? The woman just tried to arrest me!"

"I'll bet those kids sure would like to see a real bomb-sniffing dog at work."

He had me there. *I* would like to see a real bomb sniffing dog at work.

"The schedule's already been set," I said. "I don't have anything to do with that. You'd have to talk to the camp director."

"I'll get Annabelle right on it," he said decisively. "Maybe somebody from the paper can come out and take pictures. Then we'll get them to do a demo at the Fourth of July parade, more pictures, it'll make a nice spread. Good PR for the department."

Cisco and I usually did the demo at the Fourth of July Parade. "Oh that's a great idea." I didn't bother to disguise my sarcasm. "I happen to know she's terrific at arresting innocent citizens, and maybe she could shake down a few little old ladies for an encore."

He grinned. "Come on, Raine, it's not like you to hold a grudge." He changed the subject. "Speaking of the parade, did you hear Jeb Wilson is going to be the grand master?"

Jeb Wilson was our hometown boy made good, a former lieutenant govenor, now running for a national congressional seat. I didn't know him; he'd been off to college before I even started high school. But I thought I recalled that Buck had met him once or twice.

I said, "How could I miss it? It's been plastered all over the paper the last couple of weeks. What's he coming here for, anyway?"

He shrugged. "To make speeches and shake hands, I guess. It's election time."

I glanced back at the stack of posters on his desk. "Is he going to endorse you?"

"I guess so. It's a party thing."

I had known Buck all my life. We were best friends as kids, childhood sweethearts, married right out of college. I thought I knew everything about him, but I had never pictured him in this role. Running for office, making speeches, having his picture tacked up on telephone poles and posted on street corners. It felt odd, and yet somehow exactly right. I said, "I think you're going to make a good politician." I was not entirely sure that was a compliment.

He gave a crooked, self-deprecating smile. "Oh yeah? Do me a favor then and tell that to your boy-friend, will you?"

The person to whom he referred was Miles Young, Melanie's father. Since we had just returned from a family vacation together—which was one rea-son I wasn't entirely up to date on the happenings in town—there was no point in denying our relation-ship. I still wasn't entirely comfortable discussing it with other people, however, particularly with my ex-husband. The fact that Buck had brought it up made me both confused and wary. Buck rarely even acknowledged that Miles existed, and had never referred to him as my boyfriend. "What does Miles have to do with anything?"

"Aside from the fact that he's backing the other guy, not a thing."

I stared at him. "Other guy? What other guy?"

He chuckled softly, and stood. "You really do live in your own world, don't you, Raine? Come on, I'll drive you back to your car." There was a flicker of something odd across his eyes as he added, "There's something I've been meaning to talk to you about anyway."

I really wanted to pursue the subject of Miles and the other guy he was backing, but I glanced at my watch and felt my annoyance returning. "Well, make it snappy. I've got people coming to pick up dogs in half an hour. This was not on my schedule."

"It would mean a lot if you'd give Jo a chance, Raine." He opened the door for me. "She doesn't have any friends in town, and you'll like her once you get to know her. And, hey." He gave me the smile that had melted a thousand hearts. "Like your hair."

And that, right there, was why he was going to win this election.

I had to work to keep my expression sour as I stepped out into the hallway, and I have to admit my internal disposition was a lot more mellow than it had been when I'd arrived. Almost as if on cue, Deputy Jolene came around the corner, her canine partner at her side. I decided to rise to the occasion, mostly because, I'll confess it, I was still fascinated by her amazing dog.

"Hey," I said. I stepped forward with my hand extended. "I'm Raine. I guess we got off to a bad start, but welcome to town. You've got a great dog."

She stared at me as though I was something she was deciding whether or not to scrape off her shoe, and, in confusion, I dropped my hand. I turned my attention instead to the dog. "Hey, big fella," I said, leaning into him.

"Don't pet my dog," she barked sharply, and both she and the dog took a unified step backward. "He's working."

I felt like an idiot. How many times had I given that exact same lecture to school children and civic groups? You don't engage a working dog. I could actually feel my cheeks go hot, and I was about to mumble a clumsy apology when Buck touched my shoulder. "Let's go," he said.

There were a couple of dozen things swirling around in my head, ready to be spoken to him when we were alone, and I really, really wish I'd gotten a chance to say at least three of them. But as we reached the reception desk, Annabelle stopped us with, "Hey, Buck."

He paused, looking as reluctant as I was to slow down. "What?"

She looked disturbed and uncertain. "The state police just called. They found Jessie's car."

He was interested. "Yeah? Where?"

"Out on Crooked Branch Road, at the bottom of a gully."

Now even I was interested. Unless I was mistaken, that was in the middle of the National Forest, and far out of the Hanover County Sheriff's Department's jurisdiction.

Buck muttered, "Damn kids." Then, "Guess you'd better call Jessie, so he can start an insurance claim. I'll get the paperwork together. How bad was the damage?"

She looked increasingly uncomfortable. "Pretty bad," she admitted. "The state police said it was set on fire. Burned to a crisp. And Buck." Her pale blue eyes looked magnified behind the glasses as she looked up at him. "There was a body inside. They're calling it homicide."

# CHAPTER THREE

Hanover County, North Carolina, is one of those peaceful little Smoky Mountain communities that most people think exist only in the imaginations of screenwriters. We're two hours from the nearest mall, half an hour from the nearest big box store; right smack in the middle of some of the most spectacular scenery God ever put on this earth. Roaring waterfalls drop hundreds of feet off of sheer mountain cliffs into deep rock gorges. Trout flicker like silver ribbons in clear, wide riverbeds. You can hike half a day without seeing another human being and suddenly break out of a forest glade to find yourself looking down at the clouds. It is what many people call paradise, and I am one of them.

That's not to say, of course, that we are completely immune to the problems and vices of modern society. A lot of those vices are brought here by people who come here looking to escape them. According to Buck, ninety percent of the crimes in Hanover County are committed by outsiders against outsiders. The other ten percent are what you'd expect in a small, undereducated and mostly under-employed mountain community—drug-related property crimes, domestic disputes, Internet porn, the occasional crime of passion or impulse. Still, according to Buck again, Hanover County has one of the lowest crime rates in the state, and an almost one hundred percent solve rate—mostly because it's pretty hard to get away with anything when everyone knows you, your mama, your second cousin and who you spend your time with when you're not at home. For the most part, Hanover County is a quiet, peaceful place where few people bother to lock their doors and you wave at everyone you pass on the street. It is *not* the kind of place where people set cars on fire with other people inside.

I said quickly, "Anyone we know?"

While Buck said at the same time, "Any ID?" He gave me an annoyed look that was probably meant to remind me not to interfere as he stepped forward to take the message slip Annabelle held out.

"Nothing yet. I think they were hoping you could help. Here's the investigator's number."

I said, "Any missing person reports?" Generally, I would know if there were, since Cisco and I would most likely be called in to track them down. But not everyone who went missing was on foot, and not everyone who went missing was reported.

Buck shook his head absently, not looking up from the message slip. "Not lately. I guess I'd better get on this." He glanced around. "Jo, will you…"

She was front and center in a single stride, Deputy Nike a shadow at her side. Her expression was stern and her posture rigid. "Sir, request permission to be assigned to this case."

Buck replied patiently, "There is no case, Deputy. This is out of our jurisdiction."

She insisted, "Begging your pardon, sir, but the crime originated in our jurisdiction, and the prime suspect resides in this county…"

"Prime suspect?" I could not keep the amused incredulity out of my voice. "Jessie Connor?"

Even Buck's lips twitched with amusement as he explained, "Jessie is eighty-four years old and uses a walker to cross the street. The only reason he even keeps that car is so that his son can drive him back and forth to the doctor. Don't make assumptions."

I added, "Even if he could find somebody he wanted to kill, he wouldn't have the strength to do it, much less lift the body into a car and set it on fire."

Her chin lifted stubbornly, ignoring me. "Nonetheless, we should interview him."

"No we shouldn't," Buck corrected her. "The state police should. It's their case. I will send somebody out to talk to him about his car, though. Meanwhile, you can drive Miss Stockton back to her vehicle." He turned back toward his office. "And, by the way, you and Deputy Nike are on Public Education Duty this weekend. Raine'll bring you up to speed."

I shot him an outraged look but he didn't catch it. He said over his shoulder, "Annabelle, tell Wyn to check with me when she gets in, will you?"

*Wyn.* That would be the woman he had left me for.

Once, before Buck had been appointed sheriff, she had been an excellent deputy and a pretty good friend, but after the affair was uncovered it had seemed only appropriate that Wyn leave the Hanover County Sheriff's Department. Now it would seem she was back, and working for the very man she was sleeping with. That was great. Just great.

Like I said, we have our share of vices here in Paradise, and a good many of them are homegrown. This, no doubt, was what Buck had wanted to talk to me about.

I stared at his retreating back and saw his step hesitate as I said, in as neutral a tone as possible, "Wyn is back on the force?"

For a moment I thought he wouldn't answer, wouldn't even turn around. But he gave me a glance that was tight and unreadable, and he said, "Let's do this later, okay?"

I replied, "I take it back. You're not a good politician. You're an idiot." I turned to Jolene, no longer in the least bit intimidated by her or her dog. "Can we go now? I've got a business to run."

Her gaze shifted toward Buck and her nostrils flared with a breath, but it wouldn't take a genius to figure out that this was definitely not a good time for whatever it was she was about to say. She shifted her resentful gaze back to me and jerked her head toward the door. I was already striding toward it.

Both of us heard Buck's office door slam before we left the building.

I started to get into the passenger seat of the police unit, but as soon as I opened the door, Nike, the big beautiful brute, edged me out. I ended up sitting in the back like a prisoner and I could have sworn there was the ghost of a coolly triumphant smile on Jolene's lips as she opened the door for me. Well, what did I expect? With the day I was having, it seemed only right that I should take backseat to a dog.

I pressed my head back against the seat and closed my eyes, deliberately ignoring my surroundings, my driver and her canine partner. I couldn't have been more surprised when, after we'd been driving a few minutes, she actually spoke to me.

"Tell me about this Jessie Connor," she said.

I opened my eyes slowly and met hers in the rearview mirror. They were dark and piercing and accustomed to being obeyed; the kind of eyes you probably didn't want to have boring a hole through you from the other side of an interrogation table. What she no doubt saw in my eyes was resentment, pure and simple. "Why are you asking me?"

"You seem to know everything." Her gaze was on the road now. "Or think you do."

"Way to get somebody on your side," I muttered. I looked deliberately out the window.

She said, "I guess you people get a lot of bodies in burned-out cars around here."

I really didn't like the way she said "you people."
And I definitely didn't like the way she kept pushing.

I said, "Listen, I don't know where you're from
or how you got here. Maybe you miss the excitement
of the big city. Maybe you just like playing hero-cop.
But you can make things a lot easier on yourself if
you'll just settle down and pay attention to the way
things are done around here. Your boss told you to
back off. If I were you, I'd do it."

If I'd had a little milk and sugar I could have
made ice cream, the atmosphere in the car was that
cold. I could practically hear her counting to ten.
She said, "Trenton, New Jersey. That's where I'm
from. I got here via Afghanistan. So don't you worry,
I know how to take orders. I also know a thing or two
about gangland murders and organized crime. So
maybe your ex needs to learn to take help when it's
offered and deploy his resources more effectively."

Gangland murders? Organized crime? Was this
woman for real?

"Wow," I said, big-eyed. "We *are* lucky to have
you. I sure hope the state police don't try to steal
you away, because they don't know anything about
organized crime. Gee, I wonder if somebody should
tell them to look into Jessie's connection with the
mob?"

By this time we were approaching my car, and I
could tell I was coming very close to stepping over
the line—not that that had ever stopped me before.
"In the meantime, though," I said as she pulled her
vehicle off the road behind mine, "I think you'll find

Buck is pretty smart about deploying his resources effectively. For example..." I smiled and opened the car door. "You've been assigned to a kids' camp this weekend. See you there!" I waved gaily to her as I got out of the car.

The only thing I regret is that I couldn't see the expression on her face as she drove away.

# Chapter Four

I live with my three dogs in a big old farmhouse with a white columned porch at the foot of a mountain on the edge of the Nantahala Forest. A few dozen steps from my back door is Dog Daze Boarding and Training, on the site of what once was my grandparents' horse barn. Thanks to a recent remodel, I can now house twenty dogs in air-conditioned and radiant-heated comfort, with indoor training rooms and a state of the art grooming center. Next weekend every kennel would be full, but today only half a dozen dogs were waiting for their moms and dads to take them home. I screeched into the driveway barely three minutes before the first arrival.

Cisco, who had been in charge of the office while I was gone, bounded to the door on freshly trimmed fuzzy golden paws the minute he heard my car. I saw his grinning face in the top pane of the door window as I hurried up, but he dropped to all fours the minute I caught his eye because he knew he was not allowed to jump on the door. A cacophony of barking greeted me as soon as I opened the door, and Cisco, happily clutching a stuffed squirrel between his teeth, wiggled up to greet me, plumed tail waving like a flag. Mischief and Magic, the Aussies, scratched at the doors of their crates on the opposite side of the room, and when I let them out they pummeled me with bouncing paws and sloppy kisses. I dropped to my knees and gave them all hugs, inhaling their freshly washed scent and rubbing my face against their silky fur. This was always the best part about coming home.

I ushered my dogs into the play yard and returned breathlessly to the front desk just as the bell rang announcing the first pickup. The next hour was a blur of collecting dogs and dog belongings, happy reunions, cheerful good-byes, posting payments and cleaning kennels. When the last car pulled away with an excited poodle barking out of the back window, I flipped off the lights, locked the door and raced to the house. I stripped off my damp clothes, changed into fresh shorts and a tee shirt, and ran my fingers through my now dry, curly, cropped hair. It sprang back as though I'd just walked out of the salon, and I grinned at myself in the mirror. After a distinctly unpromising start to the day, all it took was some wagging tails and a good haircut to get my mood back on track.

Being a generally organized person, I had packed my duffel bag, sleeping gear and dog supplies that morning. I loaded them into the car while the dogs bounced eagerly back and forth behind the play yard fence, following my every move. They knew something was up. They had all received baths and trims that morning, because I don't take my dogs anywhere unless they're looking their very best, and now I was loading toys, backpacks and dog food into the car. This could only be good for them.

By the time I heard the greeting tap of Miles's horn and his Lexus pulled into my driveway, you'd never know that I'd spent almost an hour in police-dog custody and that, barely an hour ago, had had no hope of being ready on time. I strapped the last crate to the luggage rack, wiped my sweaty forehead as I hopped down from the running board, and waved. I can be incredibly focused when I have something pleasant to focus on, and I was looking forward to this weekend at least as much as Melanie was.

Melanie sprang out of the passenger seat as soon as the SUV stopped moving, and raced around to the backseat to untether her own dog from her seat belt. "Hey, Raine!" she called as she did so. "We're ready! I packed everything on the list! Can we go now?"

I laughed, mostly because I remembered how it was to wait so long for something you wanted to do that the prospect of waiting even another minute seemed completely beyond imagination. "I'm ready too!" I greeted her. "Let's go!"

Melanie was a plump-cheeked ten-year-old with wild dark hair and big glasses; precocious and funny and bright, whose rock-solid ambition, for the moment at least, was to train drug dogs for the FBI. How could I not like her? Her dog, Pepper, was an eight-month-old mostly golden retriever with all the goofiness appropriate to her breed and age who was completely devoted to Melanie. Her father, Miles, was a good-looking, Caribbean-tanned man with cropped spiky hair, dreamy gray eyes and rock hard muscles, although how he stayed that way I couldn't imagine because I'd never seen him lift anything heavier than a cell phone since I'd known him, and his favorite vegetable was the potato chip. Everything about him was expensive, from the way he smelled to the car he drove, although if I told him that he'd probably be surprised. He liked to think of himself as just an ordinary guy, though in fact he was one of the wealthiest men in the Southeast.

Today he did look a bit more ordinary than usual, in a paint-spattered tee shirt and jeans and a baseball cap with a hardware store logo on it. He was building a new house—along with an entire multimillion-dollar resort community—atop the very mountain that shadowed my ancestral home, and he had a tendency to be a bit hands-on about the details. The house was supposed to have been ready for occupancy two weeks ago, and it probably would have been had Miles stayed out of the way. As it was, he and Melanie were living in a luxury mobile home on the property—complete with jetted tubs, chef's kitchen, and million-dollar views—while Miles repainted trim and refinished floors that were not quite up to his exacting standards.

Pepper bounced out of the car on the end of Melanie's leash. My dogs barked their greeting from behind the fence. Miles got out more slowly, staring at me.

"Good God, Raine," he said, "what did you do to your hair?"

"Cut it," I replied, brushing my fingers across my curls. And although the expression on his face should have rendered the question moot, I added, "Like it?"

"I do!" volunteered Melanie, trotting toward me with Pepper springing and mouthing the leash beside her. "It's cool! Can I cut my hair like that, Dad?"

"You may not," he returned, still staring at me as though I were some kind of alien creature he wasn't sure he wanted to meet.

"I think it's cute," Melanie insisted.

"I don't," said her father, and Melanie gave him a light kick on the ankle, saving me the trouble of doing so. I probably wouldn't have been so gentle.

"Daaaad," she said with a meaningful roll of her eyes toward me. "You don't say that to a *girl*. Besides," she added loyally, "it *is* cute. And a lot easier to keep up with around the dogs." She gave an approving nod of her head. "I think I *will* get my hair cut."

Miles spared her a brief scowl. "Ask your mother."

That surprised me a little. Melanie's mother lived in South America with her new husband, and Miles hardly ever mentioned her. Since he had full custody, he also never deferred to her in matters of child raising, and he had already vetoed the haircut.

But because I was growing more and more annoyed with him, I did not comment.

Instead, I merely gave him a cool look and said, "Thank you, Melanie. I'm glad you like it." Then I changed the subject with a smile. "Hey, you'll never guess who I met today. A real live bomb-sniffing dog! He's the newest member of our sheriff's department."

"No kidding!" Her eyes went big. "German shepherd or Malinois?"

"Malinois," I replied, unaccountably proud of her for knowing the difference. "He speaks German and," I added triumphantly, "he's going to do a demo for us at camp!"

"Cool!"

"His name is Nike," I added. I could feel Miles examining my new haircut in the way a surgeon might examine diseased tissue. It was beginning to get on my nerves.

"She," corrected Melanie. "Nike was the winged goddess of victory. If her name is Nike, she's a she."

I lifted my eyebrows. "No kidding. I wondered why they'd name a police dog after a running shoe. How'd you know that?"

She shrugged. "Everybody knows that."

I lifted an eyebrow. "Okay then. Why don't you put Pepper in the play yard and run and get my dogs' leashes from the back porch. Your dad'll load your stuff into my car and then we'll be ready to go."

"Okay," she agreed readily, and took off toward the house at a trot.

41

"Don't let Pepper bite the leash!" I called after her.

She bent down and took the leash from Pepper's mouth, then held the leash straight above the dog's head so she couldn't reach it, just as I had taught her. I smiled with approval.

"You didn't even mention it," Miles said.

I was confused. "Mention what?"

"That you were thinking about getting your hair cut."

"Oh for heaven's sake. I didn't think about it. I just did it." Impatiently, I started toward his car to get Melanie's things.

"You might have at least asked me what I thought."

"Are you kidding me?" Now it was my turn to stop and stare. "That's the most sexist thing I've ever heard!"

"I liked your hair long."

"Do you ask me every time you get a haircut?"

"That's not the point and you know it. The point is that you didn't even take my opinion into account. You didn't care what I thought."

I was both incredulous and incensed. This was definitely not the way I had pictured the afternoon going. I thought I'd tell him about getting arrested, and he'd find a way to make me laugh about it, the way he always did. Then I'd tell him about the exotic new woman on the force, with her military background and her precision-trained dog, and he would be interested and impressed, because just about everything interested Miles. And then we'd speculate on how she'd ended up here and whether or not she had a prayer of ever fitting in, and eventually I'd casually mention that my ex-husband's girlfriend was back in town and back on the force, and I'd see the compassion in his eyes and that would make me feel better. We wouldn't talk about it now, but eventually we would, because Miles had a way of making hard conversations easy, even when you didn't want to have them. Meantime, we'd talk about camp and all the fun things Melanie and I were going to do and how much he'd miss us both... Besides, I'd really thought he'd like my hair.

"Excuse me," I said coolly, "let me get this straight. I'm supposed to ask you before I get my hair cut but you can't even bother to inform me before you throw your support behind the opposition candidate for sheriff?"

He looked momentarily taken aback. "What? What are you talking about?"

I opened the back cargo door and hauled out Pepper's overnight bag, a zippered canvas tote discretely marked with a high-end paw print logo and outfitted with multiple pockets, O-rings and hooks for necessities like treat bags and pickup bags, a built-in water bottle holder and a waterproof interior bag for kibble. I knew all this because I had helped Melanie pick it out from the pet supply catalogue. I slung the strap over my shoulder and replied shortly, "Forget it. Just get the crate, will you?"

Miles swung Melanie's sleeping bag and back-pack over one shoulder and effortlessly lifted the wire crate in its nylon holder in the other hand. He followed me to my car. "Are you trying to tell me you've decided to run for sheriff? Because that's the only reason I can think of that you'd have any interest whatsoever in whom I'm voting for."

"I didn't say 'voting for.'" My tone was short. "I said 'support.' And there are a lot of people who are interested in what you do or don't do in this election, Miles. Maybe it wouldn't hurt you to remember that not all of them are on your side, I don't care how much money you throw around. Nobody likes an outsider who comes in here trying to tell us how to run our business."

"There's the girl I know and love," he murmured.

Miles and I had been on opposite sides of every political issue that arose since the day we'd met, along with a host of other things. In fact, we had met when I headed up a committee that tried to file an injunction against him, and my name had been on at least two law suits filed against him since then. Not a very propitious start to a romance, granted, but that was who we were. There was absolutely no reason I should expect this election to be any different.

Even though his voice sounded amused, I knew he wasn't. This was just his way of getting around a fight which had somehow, at some point, become my fault. The worst part was that he was right. It wouldn't be fair to Melanie to ruin her big weekend by fighting and I certainly wasn't going to be the one who got blamed for it.

I passed him a handful of bungee ties and said, "Crate on top."

I took Melanie's backpack and arranged it in the spot I'd saved for it on the backseat floor in between Pepper's bag and my own while Miles went around the car to secure the crate. I do a lot of traveling with my dogs and am an expert packer. Transporting two humans, four dogs and a weekend's worth of supplies was a piece of cake for me. With the crates on top, I packed everything else on the floor between the bench seat and the front seat, unrolled our sleeping bags on top, attached a doggie hammock between the two seats, and created a wide, comfortable space for two dogs to lounge on the trip. Two more dogs would go in the back cargo area. I even had room left over for a rolling cart to assist with unloading when we got there, and a cooler that held Cisco's frozen food and a few treats for Melanie and me.

Miles double-checked the security of the crates and I waved at Melanie, who was in the play yard with multiple leashes draped around her neck, throwing a ball for the dogs in self-defense. "Girl assistant!" I shouted. "Release the hounds!"

She waved back and called, "Roger that!"

For some reason that reminded me of the sullen Deputy Jolene, which immediately dampened my mood. But as soon as Melanie opened the gate I was grinning again. A herd of dogs thundered toward us, tongues lolling, tails wagging, tripping and skidding in their enthusiasm, and even Miles laughed and knelt to ruffle fur and scratch ears when the four canines piled upon us, pressing their wriggling bodies close and competing for the most attention. We got them sorted out and fastened into their individual seat belts—Pepper and Cisco in the backseat, Magic and Mystery in the cargo area—and Miles said, "Are you sure you're going to be able to handle all these dogs? I can check in on the little ones if you want. I'm going to be here all weekend."

I knew he was just trying to be nice, but I rolled my eyes anyway. "You *do* know who you're talking to, right? Besides, Mischief and Magic hardly ever get to do anything. This is their vacation."

Now the glint of amusement in his eyes was genuine. "Right." He turned to Melanie. "Okay, munchkin, give me a hug." She did so, although in a rather perfunctory manner. He kissed her hair noisily and she squirmed. "Have a good time. Drink plenty of water. Don't forget the sunscreen. Don't stay up all night giggling."

"Dad!" she protested. "I've been to camp before!"

"Call me if you need anything."

"No phones until 7:00 p.m.," I reminded him. "Camp rules."

He repeated firmly, "Call me if you need anything. I'm only half an hour away."

"Forty-five minutes," I corrected, going around to the driver's side door.

"Bye, Dad." Melanie finally managed to escape his embrace and scurried into the passenger seat. "I'll call. They make you call at camp. Every night."

He smiled. "I love you, sweetie. Have fun."

"Love you back." She slammed the door and tugged at her seat belt. "I will!"

Miles came around to my door and leaned in. "Do you have everything? Is your phone on?"

"I've been to camp before, too, Dad," I said, and started the engine. Cisco panted in my ear and Pepper gave a small excited yip.

He frowned. "Don't be a smart-ass. It's a lot of responsibility, all those kids."

"And dogs," I pointed out.

"Precisely."

"Oh, for heaven's sake, Miles, there're three counselors and four instructors. That's a ratio of practically three to one. That's what you're paying for, remember?"

"It's three twenty," Melanie said, looking anxious.

I reached for the door handle.

"Don't speed," he cautioned, catching the door. "They're not going to start without you."

"I never speed," I told him, not entirely truthfully.

He leaned in and brushed my cheek with a kiss. It was more of a gesture than a genuine demonstration of affection; a girl can tell. He straightened up and closed the door, then said through the open window, "Be careful."

"Seventy-two hours," I replied impatiently, reaching for the gear shift. "We'll be back in seventy-two hours. Chill, for heaven's sake."

He thrust his hands into his jeans pockets and looked sternly back at me. "A lot can happen in seventy-two hours," he returned.

I just gave an impatient shake of my head and put the car in gear. "Bye, Miles."

"A lot!" he called after me.

Melanie and I waved out of our separate windows and shared a grin about her overprotective dad. Only later would I think back on what he had said and then I'd feel bad, because he knew exactly how much could happen in seventy-two hours. He had been with me when it had, more than once, and when I remembered that, I wished I had been nicer to him.

Hindsight is always twenty-twenty.

# Chapter Five

"The first patriots, back in 1776, met in taverns, in barns and in roadhouses," said the Professor with a small smile, "and they overthrew the tyranny of the mightiest nation on earth. I'd like to say we're mighty grateful for the use of Brother Henry's basement while we defend from tyranny the mightiest nation on earth."

He inclined a gracious nod toward their host, a middle-aged man with slightly thinning hair and bulked-up biceps and lats that he liked to show off in a USMC tee shirt that belonged to his son. Henry nodded back.

"Just think," the Professor went on, "what our forefathers might have accomplished if they'd had a Keg-o-Rator and a pool table, like we do here today." He was a charismatic man with a buzz cut and a square jaw, dressed today in pressed khakis and a polo shirt. He was a good leader, firm but fair, well liked and well respected. Some of the men claimed to know his real name, but no one actually did. Most did not care. In the chain of command, he gave the orders. That was all that mattered.

A chuckle went around the group with his remark, but it was obligatory, and did not quite break the tension. They were gathered here tonight for serious business. They all knew that.

They were fathers, husbands, deacons of the church. They were mechanics, business owners, teachers, landscapers and unemployed. Some of them had college degrees, some had barely finished high school. Most had done military service. They stayed in shape with weekend drills and once a month held practice maneuvers in the woods and gorges and bald peaks of their native land. On these occasions they told their wives and girlfriends, their bosses and employees, that they were going fishing with the guys, or leading a Boy Scout camping trip, or helping with a mission project for the church. They never regretted the lie or wavered in telling it, because their Cause was just, and because they had taken an oath.

They ranged in age from twenty-five to fifty, and they had gathered for this emergency-called meeting on a weekday evening at Henry Middleton's pleasant brick ranch at the end of Camelback Road on less than an hour's notice. Henry lived alone, his wife having left him ten years ago and his son now serving overseas, and his place was on eight fairly isolated acres. It was unlikely that anyone would notice the two dozen haphazardly parked cars and pickup trucks in the driveway and yard, but if they did he would simply invite them in, in that jovial way of his, to join the pool tournament.

They sat on ladder-back chairs and folding chairs, on the plaid club chairs and on the faux-suede sofa over which the "Don't Tread on Me" flag that was ubiquitous to groups such as theirs had been hastily tacked. A few held red plastic cups of beer, but no one was drinking. None of the men sitting in Henry Middleton's basement were under the illusion that they were here to play pool. They were here because something had gone wrong.

The Professor got to the point, his expression sobering. "Gentlemen, you know why we're here. The threat has been neutralized. I repeat, the threat has been neutralized, although not without some risk to certain of our members. We all knew what we were getting into when we signed up. Am I right?" He repeated, more forcefully, "*Am I right?*"

To which the response came with equal force, and to a man: "*Yes sir!*"

He looked around the group somberly for a moment. "The tree of liberty must, from time to time, be refreshed by the blood of tyrants and of patriots," he said. "Do you know who said that, my friends? Thomas Jefferson." And that was why they called him the Professor. He knew those things. His eyes were fierce as he said, "Remember that when the slings and arrows of the world start coming your way. We stand on the shoulders of giants to wave our flag of liberty today, gentlemen. Giants!"

The passionate murmurs of agreement that went around the room would have been cheers under other circumstances. A few raised their red cups, but no one drank.

"The mission has not been compromised," said the Professor firmly. As he spoke, he walked back and forth before the group; not pacing, precisely, but stalking. Meeting eyes. Reading expressions. Holding firm. "We are a go for July 4, thirteen hundred hours. Your orders are unchanged. Bravo squadron will execute at eleven hundred hours as directed. Alpha squadron will be in place at twelve hundred hours as directed. Charlie squadron will stand by. Are there questions?"

For a moment there was nothing, but it was clear by the way the Professor waited, his eyes searching each and every one of them with terrifying patience, that he expected something. And when it happened, it was no surprise.

A man sitting in one of the folding chairs stood. His jaw was set. He had rehearsed. "Sir," he said crisply. "Recommend the mission be postponed, sir."

Replied the Professor, "Explain, soldier."

"Our headquarters have been compromised," said the soldier. "Munitions may be in jeopardy. Security has been threatened. A police investigation may be underway. In my estimation, sir, the launch date should be reconsidered."

The Professor nodded, thinking it over. "In your estimation," he repeated, without judgment.

The soldier squared his shoulders. "Yes sir."

"I see." There was a note of compassion, even pity in his voice. The other men shifted their gazes uneasily away from the soldier who had had the temerity to speak up. "And in your *estimation*, soldier, just how should we describe our situation to High Command? Should we say we're worried, or we're scared, or we think something might go *wrong*?" He did not raise his voice, or change his posture in any way. In fact, his voice actually grew quieter, and more controlled, with each word. Only his eyes changed.

The young man swallowed hard. "No, sir," he said, forcefully. And he sat down.

The Professor looked around the assembly for a moment. "Gentlemen," he said quietly, "do you know who you are? Do you understand your power? Look around this room. *Look*!"

The last word was shouted; shouted so loud that it reverberated around the acoustically sound basement, and the men stiffened in their chairs. They looked as ordered.

"What do you see?" demanded the Professor. "Twenty men? Thirty?" His eyes were blazing now, his nostrils flared. "Wrong! You are a hundred thousand strong, gentlemen! Your brothers are lined up across this nation, waiting for you—yes, you!—to act. You hold history in your hands." As he spoke, he paced off the group, stopping with each word in front of a different individual, holding him with his eyes and his words. " Every. Single. One. Of. You."

He stood silently for a moment before them, hands clasped behind his back, surveying them all with quiet authority. He said, "We have met with challenges. But we've also been favored with fortune.

Why? Because our Cause is just. This mission will proceed as planned. I want a twenty-four-hour sur-veillance on the munitions site. The situation is not ideal, but it can be managed, are we in agreement on that?"

There was a resounding, "Yes sir!"

He nodded curtly. "Our goal is to keep civilian casualties to a minimum. We are not baby-killers. But remember how many lives have been lost already. We must have the courage to do what is necessary, and if some fall in the course of this battle, they are heroes of war, and will be honored as such. We will do what is necessary," he repeated forcefully. He squared his shoulders and held them with his gaze and demanded, "What are we, gentlemen?"

The assembly surged to its feet and responded with one voice, "We are Patriots, sir!"

The Professor smiled and dismissed his troops.

# CHAPTER SIX

Camp Bluebird is a forty-acre facility in a high valley on the northwestern side of the county, surrounded by rolling blue mountains and views that go on forever. It's been owned by the Methodist Church for over fifty years, which is the only reason such prime acreage hadn't been sold to some money-grubbing real estate developer like Miles years ago, and it's been managed for as long as I could remember by Willie Banks. He lived at the bottom of the mile-long dirt road that led up to the camp, behind a small general store that he owned and operated. Since that store was the only one for eight hard miles in either direction, and since the church paid him a salary for maintaining the camp, he did pretty well for himself. And even though the heyday of Camp Bluebird had passed ten years ago, I was pleased to see that Willie had kept it up well. After all, I was the one who'd suggested the facility to Camp Bowser Wowser when they lost their old site. I didn't want to be embarrassed.

I'd had that experience enough for one day.

The entrance was marked by a big laurel arch from which hung a sign emblazoned with frolicking cartoon dogs that read, *Camp Bowser Wowser July 1-3. Welcome!* Melanie bounced in her seat with excitement as we made the turn and the dogs, who always woke when the car slowed down, sat up and looked out eagerly through their respective windows. We drove a few hundred yards down the dirt road that was surrounded on either side by overgrown pasture land and came to a fork in the road. It had been years since I'd been here, so I was glad for the hand-lettered signs: *Lodge and Dining* (straight ahead), *Cabins* (left) *Rec Hall* (right). I drove straight.

"Now remember," I told Melanie, "no special privileges. Pepper has to sleep in the doggie dorm just like all the other dogs, even if there is room in your dorm for her tonight. No complaining."

It would have been utter chaos to have dogs bunking in the same cabins as their pint-sized owners, not to mention the liability factor should one of the children try to take a dog outside for a potty break in the middle of the night. The problem had been solved by providing a separate doggie dorm where all the dogs would be crated at night with a designated counselor to take care of their needs.

"Don't worry," Melanie assured me. "I explained to Pepper about how the fun of going to camp is sleeping away from your folks. It'll be an adventure."

I smothered a smile. "Good deal."

Registration was being held on the porch of the dining hall between five and six today for early arrivals and between eight and ten tomorrow for the regular group. There was another welcoming sign with frolicking beagles and Labs, and a small group of adults had gathered around the registration table, sipping soft drinks and chatting. I glanced at my watch and realized that, despite my best efforts, I was five minutes late for instructor orientation. "Melanie," I said, hastily unstrapping my seat belt, "I hate to run off, but they're waiting for me…"

"No problem," she said, clearly pleased to be left on her own. "I'll just walk Pepper around. What about Mischief and Magic?"

"I can keep an eye on them from here," I said. "I'll open the back door for air." I waved to the group on the porch as I climbed out. "Hi, everybody! Sorry I'm late!"

I knew the other instructors—Camp Director Margie Hildebrand and her husband Steve, who taught junior handling, and Lee Beatty, who was in charge of everything else, including the Pre-Opening Welcome Barbecue that was scheduled for tonight. As Cisco and I bounded up the steps of the low, lodge-like building, we were greeted with calls of welcome and hugs—the hugs being mostly for Cisco, I admit—and introduced to the camp nurse and vet tech, who would be coming in on a daily basis, and to the three fresh-faced teenage counselors, Andrea, Haley and Bill.

"Raine," exclaimed Margie from her place behind the registration table, "this place is marvelous! I couldn't have done better myself! It's just a little piece of heaven, isn't it? Everyone, Raine's the one who found us this place."

There were murmurs and nods of appreciation, and I was going to explain how I had worked here as a kid, but Margie is one of those steamroller personalities who lets nothing stand in way of her agenda—not a bad characteristic to have, I suppose, when you're trying to wrangle twenty five kids and twenty five dogs for three days. She went on energetically, "Now, we have five early registrations tonight who'll be here in an hour, so let's get on with it and then we'll take a quick tour. It's gorgeous, really gorgeous." As she spoke, she handed out thick manila envelopes with names and cabin numbers written on them. "Here are your tee shirts, your instructor badges, and the camp schedule, along with a list of the camp participants, their ages and dorm assignments, and their dogs. Every participant will get a copy of camp rules, which are also included in your packet. Cell phones and other electronic devices will be collected at breakfast and may be claimed after dinner each evening, lights out at ten, pick up after your dog, the usual. Remember, even though we want our campers to have fun, our primary goal is to promote a responsible, respectful relationship among all of God's creatures—and that includes counselors and instructors."

There was some laughter, and Cisco sniffed enthusiastically at my orientation packet. Apparently Margie had included dog treats—it was the kind of thing she customarily did—and I moved it out of his reach. He promptly sat back on his haunches and stared worshipfully at the envelope. It would seem someone had taught him that sitting and staring was the fastest way to get a treat. It wasn't me, I swear. I suspected Miles.

"So no sass from the campers," Margie went on. "Remember, we treat these kids like we would our dogs—firm but fair, positive reinforcement, click treat!" More laughter, and then Margie's eyes lit up and she clapped her hands together in sudden remembrance. "And good news! The sheriff's department called this afternoon to volunteer a demo by their new police dog on Saturday morning. Apparently this guy is really something, a military vet, trained in munitions, search and take-down. I can't wait to see him myself!"

As murmurs of appreciation went around the group, I muttered, "She." When Margie looked at me I explained uncomfortably, "The dog is a she."

Margie laughed. "Even better! So, this will mean pushing the Parade of Breeds back until after lunch, and the agility run-through and search demo will have to be cut short. You can take care of that, right, Raine?"

I smiled stiffly. "No problem."

"Everyone make the adjustment on your schedule. Now, a couple of special notes. Angela Bowers is allergic to peanuts, bee stings and chemical by-products—whatever that is—so she'll be wearing a red bracelet. Just make sure she has her epi-pen, counselors, before she leaves the dorm each morning. We have a couple of thunder-phobic pups..."

I glanced back toward my car and saw Magic and Mischief with their noses pressed against the back window. Melanie and Pepper were nowhere in sight and I started to get anxious until I spotted them coming up the hill from the lake. I waggled my fingers at her discreetly. She waved back and started trotting toward me. Cisco, noticing their approach, stood and swiveled his head toward them. I tightened the leash just enough to remind him that I was still there. He glanced at me, seemed to debate for a moment over his chances of securing a treat from the envelope, then compromised by sitting to watch Pepper and Melanie approach.

"All right then," said Margie, pushing up from the table, "let's take a look around. I really think you're going to like..."

Cisco stood excitedly to greet Melanie, and Pepper pulled at the leash as she galloped up the stairs toward her hero. Melanie, flushed and sweaty with running, didn't correct her, possibly because she was too out of breath. I said sharply, "Cisco, sit," which he did, even though Pepper grinned and nudged him and mouthed his ears. I restrained myself from reaching for Pepper's leash.

Instead I said, "Everyone, this is my friend Melanie."

The others smiled and started to greet her, but Melanie ignored them, pushing at her glasses as she tried to catch her breath. "Um, Raine," she managed, "there was a man down by the lake. Kind of creepy looking. He was watching us. And he had a gun."

# CHAPTER SEVEN

B uck said, "I'm real sorry to have to bring you this news, Jessie. It's a hell of a thing."

They sat on Jessie Connor's front porch, a narrow corridor with just enough room for four rocking chairs, two of which looked sturdy enough to support a man's weight. Buck sat in one of them, Jessie in the other. Jessie's walker sat to one side of his chair, his oxygen tank beside it, while Jessie, disregarding both, sucked on a cigarette. Buck, keeping one eye on the oxygen tank, had made sure he chose the chair closest to the steps.

"Blessed day in the morning," muttered Jessie, the cigarette dangling between his lips. "Burnt up, you say. Who'd do a thing like that?"

"Well, that's what we're trying to find out," Buck said. "The investigators found a couple of oxygen tanks inside the car. Makes sense they might've accelerated the fire." He paused to give Jessie a chance to make the connection between the cigarette he now smoked, and the oxygen tank at his feet. Buck saw no light go on in the other man's eyes, so he went on, "Do you normally keep oxygen in your car?"

"Now what'd I do a fool thing like that for?"

"So that would be a no?"

He drew on the cigarette. "My boy takes care of all that. You'd have to ask him."

Buck made a note. "The thing is, there was a body inside the car. We don't know who it was yet."

Jessie's eyes narrowed. "Is that a fact? Well, served him right, if you ask me. Burnt up, you say?"

Buck nodded patiently. "Yes, sir. What I was wondering is if you could remember exactly when was the last time you saw the car in your garage?"

A cylinder of ash half an inch long extended precariously from the cigarette. Buck watched it warily.

Jessie said, "Like I told you. I don't drive no more. All I know is that when my boy went to get it to drive me to town on Tuesday, it was gone."

"You son lives with you, right?"

The ash cylinder dropped harmlessly to the knee of Jessie's twill pants. He brushed it off absently with a speckled hand. "That's right."

"Where is he now?"

"At work, I reckon. He does odd jobs here and there, you know. Can't find nothing permanent since the plant closed."

Buck nodded sympathetically. "I'd like to talk to him when he gets a chance, about when was the last time he saw your car."

Jessie grunted. "Hell, I can tell you that. Drove me to church on Sunday, drove me home. Stabled her in the garage. Next thing I knew…" He stopped and frowned at the nearly dead end of his cigarette, which glowed faintly ruby. "Wait a minute. I reckon he might've taken it out Monday night, to his meeting. It was raining, I recollect, and he don't like to drive the jeep in the rain on account of the roof leaking."

Buck looked up from his notes, interested. "What meeting?"

"He used to drink, you know," Jessie confided. "Don't no more. Goes to meetings instead. Do you reckon it was one of them drunks that stole my car?"

Buck gave him a reassuring smile. "No, I don't think so."

"Well, served them right for burning up, if they did."

"Yes, sir." Buck stood. "We're going to send you a copy of the police report in the mail. You'll need it for your insurance company. It might take a week or so, though. Meantime, if your son would give me a call when he has the chance, it sure would speed things up."

"Yes, sir, I'll tell him, I surely will." Jessie let the cigarette butt drop to the porch floor and ground it out with an unsteady toe.

Buck moved closer to the steps. "You know, Jessie, you really shouldn't smoke this close to an oxygen tank."

Jessie cackled and fumbled in his shirt pocket for another cigarette. "You sound just like my doctor, son. I'll tell you what I told him. They're going to have to pry my last cigarette out of my cold dead fingers, and that's a fact."

Buck watched as he stuffed another cigarette between his lips and patted his pockets for the lighter. Buck did not feel it was his place to point out that the lighter was on the magazine-littered table beside Jessie's chair, right where he'd left it. He said instead, "There might be some other fellows by to ask you questions, from the state police. "

Jessie waved him off, still searching for the lighter. "I'll tell 'em to talk to you."

Buck started down the steps. "You take care now."

"Say, Deputy."

Buck turned. Most of the locals still couldn't remember that he was no longer a deputy, and he was used to it by now.

"Didn't I hear you was running for sheriff?"

"That's right."

Jessie finally found the lighter on the table and picked it up. He lit the cigarette and inhaled deeply. "Well, you help me get my money out of that car, and you've got my vote."

Buck said, "I appreciate that." And he even managed a smile before he turned to go back to his car.

Once there, he used his cell phone to call the office. It was the quickest way. "Say, Annabelle, do me a favor real quick. Find out when the AA meetings are held in town."

There was a silence broken only by the clack of computer keys as he started the engine and put the car in gear, beginning the three-point turn that would take him out of the driveway. She came back with, "Every other Thursday, in the basement of the Baptist church."

Buck completed the turn, his expression thoughtful as he glanced back at Jessie on the porch. Jessie lifted his hand to him. Buck returned the wave. "Yeah," he said. "That's what I thought."

He drove down the drive and made the turn onto the highway, wondering why Jessie had lied. Or, more likely, why his son had.

# CHAPTER EIGHT

"**P**robably just some hunter." Willie Banks spat a stream of tobacco out the window of the pickup as we bounced down the rutted trail toward the lake. "Or some damn fool tourist, out hiking and got lost. Holiday weekend, they come out of the woodwork." He knew as well as I did that it wasn't even close to hunting season, and possibly to keep me from pointing that out, he said, "You hear Jeb Wilson's leading the parade this year?"

I said that I had, and grabbed for the door frame as the truck hit another hole.

Margie, with her typical no-nonsense efficiency, had called Willie immediately and demanded he check out Melanie's report. The one thing that simply could not be compromised was the safety of the children, and no one—with or without a gun—had any business on this property without authorization while camp was in session. Melanie and I of course went with him, and Cisco road shotgun, tongue lolling as he hung his head out the window, drinking in the view. Pepper had stayed behind with Mischief and Magic, who were romping in the fenced baseball diamond—now known as the Puppy Games arena—under the supervision of Counselor Bill.

I asked, "How long has it been since you had a group here?"

"You all're the first one in two years," he admitted. "Recession hit, I reckon folks don't send their kids to camp like they used to. But I keep the place up, yes sir. That's what they pay me to do and that's by-George what I do."

"It looks nice," I assured him. "What I got to see of it."

"Plumbing works, kitchen's clean, roofs don't leak. That lady there, that Ms. Margie, she said make sure there's no holes in the fences, so that's what I done."

"Good. We have to be careful with the dogs."

Melanie pointed as we came over the hill that led down to the lake. "It was over there," she said, "near the woods. He was just standing there staring."

Willie Banks shifted the wad of tobacco from one cheek to the other and slid a glance at her. "You right sure about that, little lady? Could've been a shadow or something."

Melanie gave him a mildly contemptuous look. "It wasn't a shadow."

I added stiffly, because I was starting not to like his attitude, "Melanie doesn't make things up."

He didn't reply.

The lake was only about two acres, a spring-fed sheet of emerald cellophane at the base of the hill surrounded by tall cattails and scrub brush. I remembered diving off the dock into the shock of that cold water, gooseflesh tingling, squealing as catfish nibbled at my toes. I remembered canoeing across what seemed like an ocean, and tipping over in the middle—mostly through effort, not accident. The dock had rotted away and canoes were too expensive to maintain without a steady stream of campers to pay for them, but the same summer blue sky glittered overhead with a brilliance that could hurt your eyes if you looked at it too long, and the same riotous carpet of green grass spread out around the water, inviting bare feet and blankets. I was, just for a moment, transported, aching for childhood, thrilled with nostalgia and—if I were to be perfectly honest—excited about reliving it all.

I said, "Wow. Too bad about the dock. The dogs would have loved dock diving."

Melanie, momentarily forgetting her scare, glanced at me with eyes alight. "Cool," she said. "Pepper could really catch some big air."

I winked at her. "Maybe next year."

The brakes screeched as Willie brought the pickup to a halt midway around the lake line. I caught Cisco's leash before opening the door, and we climbed out. Cisco immediately went to the end of the leash, sniffing the ground, and I let him. Melanie shaded her eyes and searched the shoreline, staying close to me as we circled the truck, meeting Willie in front. He spat tobacco juice on the ground, narrowed eyes searching. "Don't see anything," he observed unnecessarily.

I ignored him and walked toward the wood line, following Cisco's lead. Melanie pointed again to the same place. "It was over there. He was just staring."

Cisco tugged at the lead, his nose to the ground, but I didn't try to pull him back. He was a tracking dog, after all, and deserved the benefit of the doubt. Besides, it's patently unfair to expect a dog to read your mind. I had not given him a command; he was on his own. Sometimes a dog just needs to be a dog.

I glanced over at Willie. "I used to work here summers," I said, trying to be friendly. "It hasn't changed much. I remember the lake used to have ducks, though. "

"Still does, winter time. No so much this time of year."

"Yeah," I agreed, "I guess not. You should see the flocks of green mallards in the autumn, Melanie. It's like a wildlife movie. These weeds produce seed pods they like to eat, and the cattails give them cover from predators." I glanced again at Willie. "Bet you have a hard time keeping the poachers off in duck season."

He grunted in reply, and stopped abruptly, staring down at the ground. He bent to pick up a faded green and red weed eater, and the weathered lines of his face smoothed as he straightened up. I followed his gaze toward the wood line, where a figure emerged, carrying a red plastic gas can.

I glanced at Melanie, but her face was impassive as she watched the man approach. He was a thin man with short pale hair in grass-stained khakis and a smudged tee shirt. Cisco lifted his head and barked, and the man lifted a hand in reply.

"It's just Reggie," Willie told me. "He's supposed to keep the grass down. I can't hardly keep up with it no more, what with my back and all."

He hadn't been doing a very good job. The weeds were up so high in places that I worried about snakes, and I kept an eye on Cisco as he sniffed around and pawed the ground experimentally, testing to see if there was anything worth digging up. The man with the gas can was of far less interest to him than the dozens of little creatures that had left their marks on the six-foot square piece of ground his leash allowed him to explore.

Melanie watched warily as the man approached.

"Ran out of gas," he explained unnecessarily when he was within voice distance. He glanced at us curiously. "Thought I had a full can in the jeep but ended up having to go down to the filling station."

I remembered that a service road encircled the property—we used to go trail riding around it when the camp kept horses—which was probably why we hadn't seen his truck. It would be closer to the lake to park on the service road than at the lodge.

"You gave the little lady here quite a scare," Willie said, and Reggie looked confused.

Melanie said, "It wasn't him."

"She thought your weed-whacker here was a gun," Willie said, handing it back to him. His tone was both relieved and amused. "I reckon it might look like one, from a distance."

Melanie repeated firmly, "It wasn't him. And it wasn't that kind of gun."

Willie looked annoyed, and I could tell Melanie was starting to get frustrated, so I spoke up. "I don't suppose you've seen anybody else out here this afternoon, have you?"

He shook his head, eyes narrowed against the sun. "Nah. 'Course, I only got here an hour ago, then I had to go for gas."

"This man had a hat," Melanie said. "And camo pants."

I noticed there was a baseball cap in Reggie's back pocket, and it could be hard to tell the difference between khaki and desert camo from a distance. "We're with the camp," I explained. "We've got a lot of kids and dogs running around here this weekend so we just want to make sure everything is safe."

Reggie glanced at Willie. "I thought that didn't start 'til tomorrow."

Cisco pranced up to me with a charred stick in his mouth, tail wagging proudly. I took it from him and he turned his attention to the newcomer, edging over for a pet. "We're with the early arrivals," I said.

Reggie grinned. "Well, don't you worry, I'll have this place all fixed up for you real nice before morning." He bent down to ruffle Cisco's ears. "Hey there, fella. I got a couple like you at home. Great duck dogs."

I tossed the burned stick into the grass while Cisco wasn't looking, and wiped my hand on my shorts. Willie said, "You better get on back to work then." And to me he said, "I told you it wasn't nothing."

Melanie looked from him to Reggie and then back to me. "But this isn't the man I saw," she said, though she sounded a little less sure of herself now. "We should look around some more."

Willie was starting to look really annoyed now, so I said, "Maybe we'll walk back up to camp. I need to exercise Cisco."

"Suit yourself." Willie strode back to the truck and in a moment we heard the engine start, the chassis squeaking and creaking as the truck backed up, turned around and started up the hill.

The sharp tang of gas fumes tinged the air as Reggie filled the tank on the weed trimmer, and Cisco wandered to the end of his leash to explore in the other direction. I said, "It's nice of you to help Willie out. He's getting up in years."

Reggie said, "I don't mind. Besides, we have a..."

"Deal?" I suggested. "Like maybe a duck season deal?"

Reggie just grinned and turned his attention back to the trimmer.

I said, "Nice talking to you, Reggie. Come on, Mel."

I gave Cisco's leash a little tug and he trotted back to me with another burned stick in his mouth. Charcoal, when chewed, makes an unholy mess on freshly laundered golden retriever fur, so I took it from him. I started to throw it away and then hesitated. I walked the few steps back to where Cisco had found the stick, and saw a cleared spot in the weeds. I kicked around the dirt until I uncovered a few more charcoal chunks. Willie had said there hadn't been a group at camp for at least a year, but the remains of this campfire were only days old.

Melanie stuffed her hands into her pockets, shoulders slumped. "I guess you think it was a weed eater I saw, too."

As she spoke, the weed eater sputtered to life and Cisco barked at it. I called him to my side and we started up the path toward the lodge. I dropped a companionable hand on her shoulder. "This is what I think. I think if we looked in Reggie Burke's pickup truck right now, we'd find a shotgun on the rack."

She looked at me in surprise.

"The way I figure it," I said, "Willie is getting too old to keep up with this big place by himself. But he can't afford to give up the caretaker's salary."

"So he hired Reggie to help him with the grass and stuff," supplied Melanie.

"In exchange for turning a blind eye if Reggie wants to hunt on posted land, which this whole camp is."

"He has duck dogs," Melanie remembered, her eyes lighting as she put it together.

"Right. And I'm guessing he took Willie's permission to hunt to mean he could hunt anything, any time. He thought the camp wasn't opening until tomorrow, so it must've scared him pretty bad when he saw you standing there watching him. So he went to put the shotgun back in the truck, picked up the gas can while he was there, and took off his baseball cap so you wouldn't recognize him."

"Yeah." Melanie nodded thoughtfully. "Nobody works out in the hot sun without a hat. My dad had his on all morning while he was on the ladder painting, and our yard men in Atlanta always wear these big straw ones."

"Right. That was the first clue. I wondered why he'd take his hat off if he was cutting grass in the afternoon sun. Also, you don't make things up."

She grinned at me and I gave her shoulder a squeeze just before I dropped my hand. "You know what else I think?"

She looked at me inquiringly.

"Maybe the less said about this to your dad, the better."

She raised her palm and I slapped it. "Mystery solved," she declared.

"Yep," I agreed. I winked at her. "Race you back to the lodge."

Cisco and I let her win, of course.

# CHAPTER NINE

One thing I have to say for Margie: she knows how to run a camp. Despite the little hiccup, we were back on track and greeting early arrivals before five o'clock. Campers were welcomed; orientation packets, paw print cookies, maps and gift bags were handed out. Dogs yapped and barked. Children laughed and shouted. The afternoon air was scented with the smell of sunshine, pine needles and charcoal smoke, and it practically made me giddy with delight. Already, I was sinking back into the glory days of my girlhood and the unpleasant events of the hours before were so far away they might never have happened at all.

I found my cabin, which was rustic but clean, nestled in a little cove down a short dirt path within the sound of a bubbling stream. There were four other private cabins on the path where the other instructors would stay, all right next to each other but shielded by trees and shrubs from view. There was a set of bunk beds, a private bathroom, and plenty of room for crates. I got my guys settled in and distributed the homemade, organic dog treats that were included in my welcome packet while Melanie and Pepper sized up their dorm mates. Later Melanie would report to me that they were all nice enough, but seemed a little dumb for their age. I assumed she meant the dogs.

I checked out the doggie dorm, which was actually the rec hall, and helped Melanie snag a prime spot for Pepper's crate underneath one of the ceiling fans. The place was huge, with twenty-foot timbered ceilings and screened transom windows all around the roofline for ventilation. The dogs should be comfortable there at night, but honestly, I did not envy the counselors who would be rotating turns sleeping there. As a kennel owner, I knew from experience that all it took was one dog who imagined he heard one squirrel, or one lonely puppy crying himself to sleep, to turn a relatively peaceful night into utter chaos. But the counselors were young; they could handle it. And that was what they were getting paid for.

There was a lot of the first-night confusion about getting dogs fed, walked and crated, but eventually we all made it to the open-air pavilion for charbroiled burgers and crispy-skinned hot dogs on paper plates with piles of chips; surely one of the best meals I've ever had. The sun was behind the trees by the time we finished, and Margie reminded everyone to walk their dogs in the designated exercise areas before bedtime, and to be sure to dispose of their waste bags in the metal containers specially marked for that purpose.

Melanie went back to the dorm to call her dad, and I took Cisco, Mischief and Magic on a last long walk before bedtime. Mischief and Magic were under excellent voice control, so they trotted by my side like two blue merle bookends, only occasionally veering off to explore a bunny path or the scent of a squirrel. Cisco, on the other hand, still had a thing or two to learn about impulse control, so he remained on a sixteen-foot retractable leash, sniffing the trail, crisscrossing his own path, snatching up sticks and pinecones and shaking them like prey, then bounding onward in search of some new adventure. There is absolutely nothing like watching a dog in his element, and I laughed out loud with the sheer pleasure of being in their company.

It occurred to me that I hadn't heard the sound of the weed eater in a while, and I turned toward the lake. So what if it meant sleeping in a cabin that smelled like wet dog all night? This was their vacation.

I called to Mischief and Magic and they galloped to my side, but Cisco, who was on the trail of something interesting, only paused and looked at me with ears raised in inquiry. I said, "Swim?" which was one of his favorite words, and he bounded toward me, grinning broadly.

We started down the path to the lake, a gorgeous cerulean and pink sunset starting to form above the tree line. In the background I could hear the occasional bark of a dog or voice of a child; otherwise, there was nothing but the crunch of my footsteps and the panting of my dogs. We had just crested the rise that overlooked the lake when my phone rang. I glanced at the ID and said, "Sorry, guys."

I answered, "Hey."

"My daughter tells me I owe you an apology," Miles said.

"Your daughter is pretty smart."

"Yeah, she tells me that too. I'm sorry I said I didn't like your hair."

That sounded a little less than sincere, so I responded in kind. "That's okay." Also less than sincere.

I noticed that the grass and weeds around the lake had indeed been cut, and the evening shadows that spread out along the wide carpet of green were deep and inviting. The dogs must have thought so too, because they started to trot ahead to explore. I let Cisco go a dozen feet or so, but warned him with a tug on the brake before he reached the end of the leash. He looked back at me reproachfully and I let him go again.

"Mel seems to be having a good time," Miles said.

"It's great here," I told him. "Ten degrees cooler than at home, easily. We'll need our sleeping bags tonight."

Small talk, careful conversation. I could tell by his silence that he had not called to talk about the weather. I watched the Aussies bound down the path ahead of me with Cisco, at the end of his leash, in the lead. I planted my weight on the back of my heels to keep from skidding as the trail descended sharply, picking up my pace a little.

Miles said, "So. I've been talking to Melanie's mother."

Never a good thing. I slowed my pace, tugging on Cisco's lead to get his attention, and said cautiously, "Oh?"

"She wants Mel to come to Brazil to visit in a couple of weeks."

"That sounds like fun." Again, I spoke cautiously, trying to figure out why his voice sounded so tight.

"The court says she gets her for two weeks every summer. Only…it seems she's not that happy with the court decision anymore. The whole custody agreement, in fact."

I felt my stomach go hollow and I stopped walking. I reached into my pocket and rattled the treat bag—I never take the dogs out without it—and three heads swiveled in my direction.

"Okay," I said, and my voice was tight now, "but she can't do anything, right? I mean, she can't really take back custody, right?" The thought of Melanie moving to Brazil left me feeling oddly wounded, preemptively bereft.

"Not as long as she stays in Brazil," he assured me. "But she can cause a lot of trouble. And since South American courts aren't known for upholding American custody agreements, I'm going with Melanie when she visits. I'm not," he added grimly, "going to let her out of my sight."

"That's a good idea." I dug the treat bag out of my pocket and Cisco galloped back to me, stopping in a perfect front sit, followed closely by the two

Aussies. I rewarded them all with bits of desiccated liver and they looked at me lovingly. I held up my hand in the signal for "stay."

"So if I was short with you this afternoon," he said, "that's why. I've been a little distracted. And pissed off."

"That's okay." I meant it this time. I sank down on the ground beside the dogs, signaled them to lie down, and they stretched out their legs until their bellies were on the ground, still watching me. I gave them more liver. The convenience of having obedience-trained dogs cannot be overstated. "What does Melanie think about the trip?"

"She's excited, and she should be. She's never been to South America before, and it's been a long time since she's seen her mom."

Now that we were friends again, the conversation was easy, and we talked for a while about Brazil and Melanie and the problems of being a single dad. Eventually I covered the phone with my hand and told the dogs, "Release." Cisco was quick to go exploring within the radius of his retractable leash, but Mischief and Magic, who can be real clowns, just rolled over and presented their bellies for me to rub. I was glad they seemed to have forgotten about the lake, which was still a hundred yards or so away.

I watched the sun turn the clouds to gold-tipped pink marshmallows while I told Miles about my adventures with the police dog Nike and her less-than-charming handler, and he found a way to make me laugh about it, as I knew he would.

"I'll be sure to take the long way to town from now on," he said. "I can tell already that is one team I definitely don't want to run afoul of."

"Yeah, well, if you do happen to run into her, be sure *not* to drop my name unless you want to end up in jail. I have a feeling I'm way down on her list of favorite people right now."

"What?" he feigned shock. "With your charm and tact? I can't imagine you alienating anybody."

That's what made me laugh. And now that we were friends again, I asked casually, "So who is the other candidate for sheriff, anyway? And why didn't I know about him?"

"You've been a little over your head since we got back from the beach, sugar," he replied. "You told me yourself you haven't read the paper in three weeks. And given the size of this county's paper, that's just plain pathetic."

He was right, of course. I'd been out of town at dog shows two weekends in a row, and it always takes three days to catch up after a show. Trying to run the kennel by myself had left me too exhausted to do anything but fall into bed after supper, and I'd barely had time for more than a cursory phone call to my aunt or my friends. When we talked, it was not about politics.

"His name is Marshall Becker," Miles went on, answering my question. "He worked for the sheriff's department here for five years, then moved to Nashville, where he was on the police force for twelve years. I like him. He's got some progressive ideas. You're not really mad at me for supporting him, are you?"

Marshall Becker. The name sounded familiar. I'd have to get the details from Uncle Roe. "No, I'm not mad. But I thought you liked Buck."

"I've got nothing against him. Except for the way he treated my girl, of course."

It took a minute to realize he was talking about me. "Oh, come on, Miles, you wouldn't really..."

"Of course not. I don't make political decisions for personal reasons. The guy asked me for a campaign donation and I obliged, that's all."

"So if Buck asked for a donation, you'd give it to him, too?"

His silence was telling, and I was surprised. Miles was the kind of man who knew the value of hedging his bets, and it wasn't like him to take sides in a fight in which he had nothing to gain. My attention quickened.

I said, "Miles? Is something going on I should know about?"

He sighed. "You want the truth, right?"

Now I was worried. I said, "Right." Even though I wasn't sure I meant it.

"The truth is," he said, "I really, really don't like your hair. But I'm pretty crazy about the rest of you, so let's not get into a fight over politics, okay?"

I pulled a face. "Get over the hair. I don't care whether you like it or not." A partial truth. "And I don't have a horse in this race. As far as I'm concerned, if Buck loses this election it's his own damn

83

fault." I wasn't ready to talk about the girlfriend he had brought on the force, but I wondered if Miles already knew. "I'm just curious, that's all. What set you against him?"

I had been vaguely aware of Cisco, nosing and pawing at something in the weeds a dozen or so feet away, which was hardly unusual for him. Now he brought me his treasure, paws prancing, tail wagging. I glanced at it, but it didn't appear to be alive or dangerous, so I ignored him for the moment, focusing on Miles.

This time the silence was a little longer. "Nothing against your boy," he said at last, "but I'm not wild about the company he keeps. And he needs to know that if he's in bed with Jeb Wilson he'd better watch his back."

I frowned in confusion. "What?" Cisco edged between Mischief and me, demanding attention, and I put an arm around his shoulders, patting him absently.

"Baby, you've got a big day ahead teaching kids and dogs how to behave themselves. Get some rest. I'll call you tomorrow. And make sure Melanie wears sunscreen, will you? She always forgets."

"Yeah, okay," I said, still uneasy. I drew a breath for another question but he cut me off.

"Sleep tight, sugar. Don't let the bears and wolves bite."

That made me smile. "'Nite, Miles."

I put the phone away and finally turned my attention to Cisco's treasure. By this time he had stretched out on the ground with his find between his paws, preparing for a nice long chew, and he wasn't nearly as excited about sharing with me as he had been earlier. I took the prize anyway. It was an athletic sock, oddly enough still fairly close to white, and for a moment I thought some camper had lost it. Then I realized it was too big to belong to a child, and I wondered if for some reason Reggie had taken off his shoes and socks this afternoon, maybe to swim in the lake after finishing the grass. At any rate, it was not something I wanted to hold onto, so I tossed it back in the general direction from which Cisco had taken it, hoping it would land near its mate.

Naturally, Cisco wanted to chase, but I brought him up short, standing and calling all the dogs to my side. It was getting dark, and I was not quite as comfortable being here alone as I had been a few moments ago. "Come on, guys," I said, and my eyes darted quickly toward the wood line, "let's go."

Besides, Miles was right. We all had a big day tomorrow.

# CHAPTER TEN

Iwas up with the first trill of birdsong the next morning, flinging aside the downy warmth of my sleeping bag and springing from my cot with barely a stretch to mark the passage of an absolutely blissful night's sleep. I love camping. I love the smell of the woods and the sound of gurgling streams, the cool damp taste of mountain nights and the gentle music of tree frogs and crickets. I never sleep more soundly than when I am out in the woods, even when the woods are complemented by indoor plumbing and electricity.

The last dormitory dog had not quieted down until shortly after midnight, and at this barely dawn hour none of them had stirred yet. I didn't dare take my own crew up the hill to the exercise area and risk waking the whole camp, so after they gobbled their breakfast I took them for a quick run in the opposite direction, back toward the lake. Morning clouds were rising over the deep blue mountains in tendrils and wisps, and as the sun slowly painted the sky pink and azure, we saw a deer darting through the woods. I kept a tight hold on Cisco's leash; disaster averted.

I fell into an easy rhythm, losing myself in the crunch of my running shoes on hard-packed dirt, the sound of my breath and the counterpoint of the dogs' panting. The air was cool and earthy, scented by the lingering wood smoke smell from last night's barbecue, and a heavy dew dripped from branches overhead. There is nothing sweeter, more ripe with possibilities and joyous, explosive life, than the still-ness of a mountain morning.

That was what I was thinking—or perhaps some-thing equally as poetic—when my reverie was sud-denly shattered by Cisco's abrupt and, as far as I could tell, completely uncalled-for barking fit. He stopped about ten feet ahead of me on his long leash, feet planted, ears forward, tail curved over his back, gaze fixed on something beyond the lake, barking furiously. I almost tumbled head-over-heels in my effort to keep from skidding into him. He barked, the Aussies joined in—even though I could swear they had no idea what they were barking at—and, because I'm no fool and I know that well-social-ized dogs like mine don't bark at nothing, I stopped to scrutinize my surroundings. The Aussies circled, barking at nothing at all, but Cisco remained firm, his deep-throated bark and focused gaze insisting that all was not as it should be. I could not have heard anything above the cacophony even if there had been something to hear. My breath was coming hard and my heart was going perhaps a beat or two faster than its normal running rhythm. I could feel my scalp prickle with alarm as I scanned the wood line, the lake, the horizon beyond, and I saw absolutely nothing out of the ordinary. Until, abruptly, the center of the lake erupted like a water spout.

A bass, easily ten pounds, exploded out of the water, snatched a bug from the air, and dropped back again, leaving a cascade of ripples in its wake. I laughed out loud with relief and delight, tugged on Cisco's leash, and commanded, "Dogs! Quiet!"

It was too late, of course. As we jogged back up the trail toward the camp, I could hear the voices of the dormitory dogs happily joining in the morning chorus, and I winced with silent apology to the sleeping campers. On the other hand, it was almost six o'clock. Time for them to get up anyway.

Only later did I realize something else; we had not had a wood fire at the barbecue last night, and even if we had, I shouldn't have been able to smell the smoke at the lake.

The camp cook served us cinnamon French toast with strawberries and maple syrup, hash browns and bacon while Margie went over the schedule. The actual pint-sized campers would of course be served a more allergen-free/gluten-free/vegan-appropriate version of the meal. I was profoundly grateful to be a grown-up as I helped myself to a second serving of French toast.

While we ate, Margie went over the day's schedule, ending with, "Mr. Banks has already set up canopies in all of the fields for shade, and he'll be going around on his ATV during the day delivering fresh water and dog treats. He's even got a wagon hooked up in case anyone needs a ride back to the lodge, but let's try to discourage the kids from abusing his hospitality, shall we? I understand it rains here just about every afternoon…" She glanced at me and I wrinkled my nose, nodding confirmation. "So have a backup plan if your class gets interrupted by a downpour."

Margie began to slide walkie-talkies across the table to us. "Their range is pretty limited," she explained. "The nurse is on Channel One, vet tech on Two. Seriously, friends, do not be afraid to press those buttons. That's what we're paying them for, and the safety and comfort of our campers are our first priority. The other instructors' channels are marked on the devices."

I was studying my radio when she placed her hands atop the table and declared quietly, "Ladies and gentlemen, you are here because you are the best in your field. I can't begin to compensate you, or thank you, enough for your service. I hope you will take satisfaction in the fact that a whole new generation of dog lovers will go forward from here to spread our message of responsibility, equality and love."

As a matter of fact, I did.


Eager to be reunited with their dogs, our early registration campers were up, breakfasted and out walking their dogs before the new registrants arrived. I was happy to see Pepper had come through the night in good spirits, and was bouncing happily along beside Melanie as she walked along the path between the dormitories. I was on my way to set up the agility field with Cisco by my side, and Pepper lost her impulse control when she saw him. Melanie set her heels like I had taught her, waited until Pepper realized her mistake and came back to her side, and then rewarded her with a piece of bacon from breakfast. Of course the kids had all been told to bring training treats from home, but Melanie knew the value of a high-value reward, and we all turned a blind eye to pilfering from the buffet for a good cause.

I put Cisco in a sit and watched with approval as Melanie walked Pepper over to us in a pretty close to perfect heel, guiding her with bacon and voice approval. I would be very much surprised if she didn't win a blue ribbon in the Puppies Under One Year Old group in the obedience trial on Sunday—if in fact she didn't win Best in Show—but I didn't say anything to her. She was pretty full of herself already, and I hadn't really had a chance to size up the competition.

I did say, "Good job, Pepper! That's hard to do with so many dogs around."

Melanie grinned. "Not really. She'd rather have bacon."

Cisco shifted his feet and licked his chops as the scent of bacon came closer, and I tightened my hand on his leash, reminding him he was in a sit. "What group are you in?"

"B," she said. "I get Obedience with you this afternoon and agility in the morning. I think I'll blow off Junior Handling, though," she added, "since I'm not going to show Pepper in conformation."

As an instructor, I knew I should point out the value of every class, but when I thought about how many classes I'd blown off during my school years, I was afraid it might sound a bit hypocritical. Particularly since I privately agreed with her.

I said, "Tell you what. I'm on my way to set up the agility field. If you'd like to help, maybe we could take the dogs for a swim during the Junior Handling class." After all, I had promised Cisco a swim last night, and I did want to have a closer look around the shore before all the kids arrived.

"Sure!" She released Pepper from her heel and kept her from lunging at Cisco by feeding her the rest of the bacon. That kid was really sharp. "What are we waiting for? Pepper loves to swim!"

As we walked to the soccer field, she told me about the bone-shaped pool at Pepper's day care in Atlanta, and how she had tried to talk her dad into putting something similar in their mountain house.

"I don't think he's going to go for it, though," she confided as we reached the soccer field where the ring gating and agility equipment were stacked under blue tarps. "He says there's already an indoor and outdoor pool at the clubhouse and it's too late to make them bone shaped."

"Wow," I said. "Indoor and outdoor." I had never seen, nor wanted to see, the fancy club house Miles was building on the site of what once had been one of the most breathtaking valley views in the county. I supposed it still was a breathtaking view, of course. The only difference was that now it would not be enjoyed by hikers and hunters, but by golf-playing millionaires and their chardonnay-sipping wives who gazed out over the valley in air-conditioned comfort through panes of storm-rated glass. The whole thing threatened to depress me, so I changed the subject.

"Guess you're going to miss Atlanta when you guys move up here full time," I said.

She shrugged. "Not really. I haven't been there that long. And Dad says the school up here is a lot better." She grinned at me. "They have horseback riding as a regular class!"

Miles had enrolled his daughter as a day student in an exclusive private boarding school half an hour away; the public education our little village had to offer being completely out of the question. If horseback riding was on the curriculum, I could definitely understand why.

I said, "They used to have horseback riding here when I was a kid."

"Oh, yeah? What was it like back then?"

She made it sound as though she pictured covered wagons rumbling along in the background. "Not that much different. No dogs, though."

"What did you do?"

"The usual. Canoeing on the lake, swimming, soccer, arts and crafts…" I smiled a little to myself. "Smooching with my boyfriend." I realized too late that might not be an appropriate thing to say to a ten-year-old, so I added quickly, "Of course, I was a lot older then. I was a counselor, almost grown up."

Melanie was sanguine. "Whatever happened to him? Your boyfriend, I mean."

I made a small wry face. "Actually, I married him."

She looked interested. "Sheriff Buck?"

I nodded. "Let's set up the ring gating first, then we can let the dogs loose." Meantime, I clipped the dogs' leashes to one of the spiral ground stakes that were provided for that purpose, and handed her a couple of the folding plastic gates, picking up an armful for myself. "Let's start here and work our way out."

She said, "I guess your hair was short back then."

At first I didn't follow. "What?"

"When you met Sheriff Buck. I guess your hair was short."

I thought back, carrying the gates across the grass. "I guess so." I set up the first gate, and she snapped hers in place beside mine. She had done this before.

"It was long when we met you," Melanie said. "My dad and me."

I snapped another gate next to hers. "What, my hair?"

"Yeah. It was long."

"I guess it was." And then I said. "Oh." I looked at her with slow understanding and a small smile. "Yeah, it was long. "

She shrugged. "Sometimes it takes my dad a while to get used to things. It took him a couple of months to get used to me. So, are we doing a regulation ring or what?"

She really was the coolest kid ever.

When the field was enclosed by ring gating, I unleashed Pepper and Cisco to wander at will. This meant that they ran in wild pointless circles for the first thirty seconds, and Melanie and I watched them, laughing. Pepper clearly had a case of hero worship, and Cisco, being a generally good-natured dog with absolutely no self-esteem issues, accepted it as his due. He allowed Pepper to chase him and even to catch him, but as soon as she drew abreast he turned and started chasing her. They raced around the ring until Cisco abruptly lost interest and started sniffing the ground. Pepper looked disappointed for a moment, then pretended not to care, bounding away in search of her own amusements.

I dragged the six-foot tunnel to the center of the ring while Melanie put together the offset weave poles and jumps. She had a set of similar equipment in her backyard at home and knew where everything went. While we worked, Melanie told me about her dorm mates—Alexandria with the Labradoodle, who was cute but couldn't be trusted off leash; Bailey, who looked just like her Bichon but wasn't nearly as smart; Monty—short for Montana—whose Great

Pyrenees puppy was already bigger than she was. I had noticed that pair coming in and wondered if the short blond girl was going to be able to handle the huge dog, but Melanie assured me the dog was just a great big teddy bear. I couldn't help smiling at her authoritative assessment of her fellow campers, and was glad she was settling in so well. When I was her age it had taken me more than one night to feel comfortable in a new place. But then again, Melanie at age ten was already a more experienced traveler than I would ever be.

With the two of us working, it only took moments to set up a puppy practice ring—a low tire jump, three bar jumps, weave poles, tunnel and a low dog walk. "Can I take Pepper through?" Melanie wanted to know. "Since we don't get to take agility until tomorrow?"

"Sure," I said. Since she had given me the teacher's advantage with the lowdown on her dorm mates, it was the least I could do. "On leash, though, just like you were in class." The important thing, when training a new dog in agility, was to make sure the pup took every obstacle the first time, and to reward appropriately when she did. That was hard to do when the puppy was running wildly off leash in the opposite direction.

She made a sour face. "She doesn't need a leash."

"Maybe not, but I'm the teacher."

"I'll raise the bars," she decided. "Pepper can jump way higher than that."

"Not on leash she can't. Safety first."

Melanie gave me an eye roll and went to get Pepper's leash, scuffing her feet a little to show her disagreement with my edict. She's not *always* a perfect child.

The two goldens had long since lost interest in what we were doing, and were gathered at the opposite end of the ring, pawing and sniffing at the ground. This is never a good sign, since whatever is uncovered beneath a layer of dirt or grass is probably not going to be good for either my dog's digestion or for my clean white shorts once I removed it from his mouth. I called sharply, "Cisco!" He looked up at me as I started toward him, then turned back to his explorations.

I said again, "Cisco, Pepper! Stop that!" And Pepper, the little imp, suddenly snatched something from the ground, did a half-spin, and took off running with her prize.

I called to Melanie, "She has something in her mouth!"

Melanie got down on her knees, held out a piece of bacon, and called "Here, Pepper!" Pepper made an about turn and was sitting in front of Melanie munching bacon by the time I reached them.

Melanie snapped on Pepper's leash and stood, holding out a small metal tube in her hand. "Good thing you saw her," she said. "She could have swallowed this."

I took the object from her, frowning. "Yeah," I said, and glanced over at Cisco, who had broadened his search but was still sniffing the ground. "I'd better make sure there aren't any more."

Cisco, not to be outdone by the little upstart Pepper, pranced over to me with his butt wiggling and his teeth clenched around another metal cylinder. Unlike Pepper, however, he dropped it into my hand on command, and *then* sat grinning at me expectantly, waiting for his treat. I dug into my pocket for the plastic bag of freeze-dried chicken and tossed him his reward.

"What are they?" Melanie asked as I gazed at the two objects in my open palm.

"Shell casings," I replied, glancing around thoughtfully.

"Maybe the hunter we met at the lake yesterday?" she suggested.

"Maybe," I agreed. Except that hunting season, even the illegal kind that was performed on posted land, had been over for six months. The brass casings I held in my hand were barely even dirty.

We scoured around and found a dozen or so brass shells, all within a six-foot radius. I stuffed them in my fanny pack, because I really didn't want to take a chance on any of the puppies picking them up, and stood for a moment near the edge of the ring, scanning the surrounding terrain until I saw what I was looking for. I snapped on Cisco's leash, picked up one of the PVC weave poles to use as a walking stick, and told Melanie, "Wait here just a sec."

I walked a few dozen yards into high grass, swinging the weave pole in front of me to scare away small creatures, until I came upon the broken bale of hay, slightly damp from yesterday's rain and hastily scattered. Cisco sniffed curiously, but didn't find anything interesting. I poked around with my pole, turning over clumps of hay, until I saw a smear of red.

"What's that?" Melanie said at my elbow.

I jumped. "What are you doing here? There could be snakes!"

"You scared them all away," she said, unconcerned as she peered around me to examine the pile of hay. Pepper bounded forward to chew Cisco's ear, and he ignored her. "What is it?"

"A target," I said, pointing at the smudges of red paint on the clumps of hay. "Somebody's been target shooting out here, that's all."

"I'll bet it was that guy with the weed eater."

"You're probably right." The only thing was, I had been around guns all my life, and those casings didn't look as though they belonged to any handgun or rifle I had ever seen.

I glanced at my watch. "Come on, show me what Pepper can do. And then we'll have to hurry if we're going to be on time for orientation."

"Yeah," she agreed, "Counselor Bill said those of us who got here last night are supposed to kind of be in charge of the others, show them around and stuff." Melanie liked to be in charge. "So we'd better hurry."

I chuckled as she and Pepper trotted back to the ring, Cisco watching alertly after them. I dug the shell casings out of my pack and tossed them as far into the weeds as I could, out of the reach of curious dogs. I saved one, though, to show to Buck when I got back. I wasn't entirely sure why.

# CHAPTER ELEVEN

Wyn had convinced Buck shortly after she agreed to come back to the department that being seen together outside the office while in uniform was a really bad idea, at least until after the election was over. That meant they didn't have meals together while on duty, even though he often had lunch or breakfast with the other deputies during the day. They didn't pull their vehicles close in parking lots to catch up on business or just pass the time as he did with the other guys. They did their communicating by phone or radio, where anyone could hear. And most annoying for him, they never interviewed witnesses together, gathered evidence together, or examined scenes together, even when they were working the same case—which was most of the time. Wyn was the best partner he'd ever had, back when they had both been deputies and ridden together. She saw things he didn't, and some of his best thinking had been done out loud, to her, riding the roads and patrolling the highways of Hanover County. She was still the best partner he'd ever had, and he still did his best thinking out loud to her, only these days, most of the time it had to wait until they got home.

That was why he was surprised to see her come into Miss Meg's Diner a little after seven in the morning, glance around until she saw him, and then start his way. The diner was busy with the bustle and clatter of the breakfast crowd: the smell of coffee and eggs, the rattle of dishes, the buzz of voices. Buck had taken his coffee over to Buddy Hall's table, who was head of the Chamber of Commerce, and had scheduled a meeting with him later that day to talk about the parade schedule. They were both glad to save themselves the time, and they got the last minute details on the parade schedule ironed out while Buddy finished up his pancakes and Buck waited for his toast and eggs.

"The only thing is," Buddy was saying, "we're going to need to close Main Street for about an hour tonight to get those big banners up over the reviewing stand. Generally, we'd do it the night before but with it falling on a Sunday and all we couldn't find anybody to drive the cherry picker unless it was tonight. Sorry about the short notice."

Buck nodded. "As long as it's after closing time for the stores there shouldn't be much of a problem. I've got Jeb Wilson's people coming Sunday anyway to check out the parade route, so it'll be better to get as much set up in advance as we can. I'll send a couple of patrol cars over. Call me when you know what time you can get the cherry picker because we

101

can't reroute traffic more than an hour. It's Friday night, you know. "

"I'll check as soon as I get back to the office." Then he grinned. "It sure is something about old Jeb, isn't it? Whoever would've thought he'd amount to anything? But folks sure are worked up about him coming to town."

"Yeah, I guess," Buck agreed, and that was when he saw Wyn.

She was working a week of nights—it was her turn in the rotation—and had that weary, just-coming-off-shift look common to all night shift workers. Her dark bun was a little messy, her uniform tired, and her eyes looked puffy and sun-shocked. Buck had worked plenty of night shifts himself and knew the feeling.

She said, "Morning, gentlemen," as she approached and Buck started to stand up.

"Everything okay?"

She waved him back down. "I didn't mean to interrupt. I saw you through the window and thought I could save myself some paperwork by giving you my report in person. But if you're busy…"

"Just finished," Buddy assured her, tossing back the last of his coffee as he stood. "You all go on with your business. Let's get somebody over here to clean up these dishes." He waved at the waitress who was already on her way over with Buck's order. He slipped her a couple of dollars as she gathered up his dishes and wiped the table with a cloth. "Buck, good seeing you. Glad we got this out of the way. Ma'am…" He nodded at Wyn. "Have a good day."

Wyn slid into the chair Buddy had vacated and the waitress said, "Back with coffee in a minute, hon."

Wyn started to protest, then shrugged. The waitress was already gone.

Buck speared his eggs, watching her. "Must be important."

"Kind of." She frowned a little. "Maybe. I just thought you'd want to know. Les and I happened by the White Lightning Saloon last night—bar fight, didn't amount to anything, the report's on your desk—and guess who happened to be sitting there at the bar sipping whiskey like it was soda water? Reg Connor."

Buck spread jam on his toast. "Fell off the wagon, did he?"

"Right." Absently she reached for a piece of bacon from his plate. "Like there's ever been a wagon to fall off of. That man's never been to a meeting in his life."

"Particularly one that's held on Monday night," Buck reminded her. "I called around to every AA group in a hundred miles. A few on Tuesday, lots of Fridays, no Mondays."

Wyn crunched down on the bacon. "So it seemed like a good chance to talk to him about what he was doing Monday night, since we know he wasn't where he told his father he was, and whether he might have any ideas about the identity of the victim in the car, or failing that, whether he might have any ideas about who might want to steal his father's car and set it on fire."

Buck took another forkful of eggs while the waitress brought Wyn's coffee. She patted Wyn's shoulder just before she left and said, "You gonna want some breakfast, honey, or do you two want to share?"

Wyn glanced guiltily at the bacon between her fingers and then put it down quickly on her coffee saucer, blushing. "I'm not staying," she said.

"Holler if you change your mind." The waitress sailed off to her next table.

Buck said, amused, "There's no extra charge for sharing. You want some toast, too? I've got plenty."

She scowled, her blush deepening. "This isn't a date. Everyone is staring."

Buck glanced around and no one, as far as he could tell, was staring. He said, turning back to his eggs, "Speaking of dates, when are we going to have one?"

She sat back in her chair, her shoulders stiff. "That is completely inappropriate."

He moved his gaze deliberately to her hand. "You're not wearing it."

"I told you, not at work."

"Wyn," he said patiently, "everybody knows about us. The guys at the department know about us. Buddy Hall knows about us. The waitress knows about us. What's not appropriate about being honest?"

She said, "Have you talked to Raine yet?"

Silence was her answer, and a quick shifting of his gaze. Her lips tightened, and she, too, looked away for a moment. The silence lingered.

Then he picked up his coffee cup. "All right," he said. "Go on. What did you get out of Reggie?"

Her expression settled into thoughtful lines, and she picked up the bacon again. "It was the weirdest thing," she said. "He just kind of laughed and shook his head and he said, 'You think that's your biggest problem, Deputy?' or something like that."

Buck lifted an eyebrow. "That drunk, huh?"

She shook her head. "I don't think so. At least not from what I could tell. The bartender said it was his first. Of course, we don't know how much he had before he got there but...no. He didn't seem drunk to me. It was just like...I don't know. Weird." She frowned and crunched down on the bacon. "Then he seemed to get with the program and said that he hadn't been anywhere Monday night, that his dad was confused, medication, blah, blah, and as far as he knew the car hadn't been driven since Sunday church. He said the bedrooms are on the back side of the house and they wouldn't have heard anything if someone came in the middle of the night, and the first time he noticed it was gone was when he phoned in the report. About what you'd expect. And then—this is the interesting part—when I asked if he had any idea who the victim might be, the one who was found in his dad's car, he got real quiet and just kind of stared into his drink for a while, and then he said, 'Nobody worth knowing.'"

Buck looked at her, his attention quickening.

"That's what he said. I wrote it down, and Les was with me. 'Nobody worth knowing.'"

Buck frowned. "That is interesting." He put down the last piece of toast. "I checked on the preliminary forensics last night before I left. It was definitely a homicide. The victim had a forty-four caliber bullet hole in his skull, dead before the fire."

Wyn took a breath. "Wow. If we were TV cops, we'd be hauling Reggie in for questioning right now."

"At the very least."

"I wonder if he knows that."

Buck said, "I wonder if he cares."

Wyn said, "It's not our case."

"No evidence, anyway."

She picked up her coffee cup. "Yeah, but I've got a bad feeling."

"Yeah," agreed Buck, "and I think I'll give that state investigator a call, maybe point him in the right direction."

"The thing is," speculated Wyn, sipping her coffee, "until we know who the victim is, we can't begin to come up with a motive."

"But if we had a motive," Buck countered, "we might be able to figure out who the victim is."

Wyn was thoughtful, sipping her coffee. "Nobody local."

"Probably not. Someone would've come forward with a missing person's by now."

"Which is why it's not our case."

"Among other reasons." Buck's phone vibrated in his shirt pocket and he took it out, glancing at the caller ID. "Speak of the devil," he murmured. He pressed the button and answered, "Lawson."

"Sheriff, this is Pete Bennet, state police." The voice sounded wary, not quite as comradely as it had been in previous conversations. "We might've caught a break on this vic in this car burning. Nothing for sure yet, still running it through the databases, but there was a cell phone in the car...could've been his, could've belonged to the perp. We were able to retrieve enough of the serial number to come up with a name. Carl Brunner. Mean anything to you?"

Buck frowned. "Not off hand. I'll do some checking when I get back to the office."

Bennet gave a small grunt of consent. "We just got in a record of the last week's phone calls. One number showed up twice—incoming and outgoing. Turns out it belongs to a deputy of yours. One Jolene Smith. We'll be talking to her, of course. But I just thought you'd like a heads-up."

As he spoke, Buck's face grew stiller, and the lines around his lips grew tighter. Wyn put down her coffee cup, watching him.

Buck said, with an effort, "I appreciate that. Do me one more favor if you will. Give me an hour. Let me see what I can find out."

"I was hoping you'd say that. It'll take me that long to get out there anyway." The last word was broken by a buzz on the other end of the line. "Hey, hold on a minute. That might be my confirmation on the ID."

While he was on hold, Buck turned the mouthpiece to his jaw and told Wyn tersely, "They think they have an ID on the victim. Carl Brunner. Familiar?"

She shook her head. "Do you want me to check into it?"

"You may not have to." The knot between his brows deepened. "Seems our own Deputy Jo might have known him pretty well."

Her eyes flew wide. "*What?*"

But Buck turned his attention back to the phone as Bennet came back on the line. "Sheriff, looks like we both just saved ourselves some trouble." The words were innocuous, but his voice was tight with frustration. "Seems like that name triggered something on a federal database. They're taking over, and I'm spending the weekend barbecuing and watching fireworks. Hope you get to do the same. But Sheriff," his tone grew somber, "I'd keep that deputy under watch if I were you. I've got a funny feeling she'll be getting a visit from a man in a suit before long."

He disconnected, and Buck put the phone back in his pocket, his expression distant and preoccupied.

"What?" Wyn demanded.

He looked back at her, still frowning. "Our stolen car just became a federal case," he said. "And I'm going to find out why."

Wyn said, "Federal? Why?"

"Gotta go." He stood abruptly and dropped a ten-dollar bill on the table. He barely stopped himself before bending to kiss her absently. Instead he gave her a wry apologetic smile. "Fill you in later. Thanks for stopping by. Get some sleep."

She lifted her empty coffee cup and replied, "Fat chance of that."

But he was already gone, and the bell that clanged on the door that shut after him had a particularly angry sound.


It took him five minutes to get to the office. The change of watch was in progress; night duty going off, day shift coming on. He waved off the night commander with his report, he ignored the messages that were thrust at him, and when his deputies, oncoming and off-going, saw the expression on his face, they got out of his way. He found Jolene getting ready to go on patrol and he said to her brusquely, without stopping, "My office."

She looked surprised, but put Nike in a down-stay under her desk and followed him. When she crossed the threshold, he said, "Close the door."

She complied, and he stalked behind his desk then turned to face her. "Who is Carl Brunner?"

Her face changed, muscles going slack, eyes growing dark. She sat down.

He placed his palms on the desk and leaned forward, his anger, deep and quiet, boring down on her. "And who the hell," he demanded coldly, "are you?"

It took a moment for her to reply. "It was him then?" She looked shaken, or as shaken as it was possible for a woman with completely inscrutable features to look. "In the car, it was Brunner?"

Buck said distinctly, "Answer my question."

Her lips compressed. She looked momentarily uncertain. Then she said, "I need to make a phone call."

"Put it on speaker."

He sat down behind the desk but didn't take his eyes off her. She took out her phone and dialed a number. A man answered with a curt, "Manahan."

Jolene held the phone away from her face, mouthpiece pointing toward her. "Agent Manahan, this is Jolene Smith. I have Sheriff Lawson here. He asked me to put you on speaker."

There was barely even a hesitation. "Yes, Sheriff. I've been expecting to hear from you."

Buck had no idea whether that was true or not. "What agency are you with?"

This time the hesitation was distinct, ringing with things carefully left unsaid. "I'm with the FBI, Sheriff, Charlotte Field Office."

Buck frowned. He was accustomed to dealing with the Asheville office, the resident agency that served the western mountains. If they were sending a guy from Charlotte, something big must be going on, and he had a bad feeling it was connected with Jeb Wilson's visit. Manahan's next words only made that bad feeling worse.

"I'm on my way down with members of the task force to fill you in. Meantime, Officer Smith can tell you what she knows. I'm not comfortable going any further on the phone. Officer Smith?"

"Yes, sir. Thank you."

She disconnected and put the phone away. Buck glared at her, his back teeth clenched against the volcano of temper that was so close to eruption he could taste ashes on the back of his tongue. Jolene felt his fury and her nostrils flared, shoulders squaring in self-defense.

"My employment contract states that I, and I quote, 'may in case of a national emergency or as need demands be conscripted into service by other law enforcement agencies of the United States government,'" she said. "I was only following orders."

"Your contract also states that I can fire your ass for cause any time I see fit," he returned shortly, "and from where I'm sitting I've got plenty of cause. Who was Carl Brunner?"

She pressed her palms flat on the knees of her uniform trousers. The gesture might almost have been construed as nervous. "I didn't know him," she said. "My understanding was that he was working undercover in the area with a group of dissidents. When I was assigned here I was told I would be his local redundancy contact. A redundancy contact is—"

"I know what it is." Buck scowled at her. "A Hail Mary when everything else fails. Only to be used in an emergency."

She nodded. "I was given a number to call and I did. He called back with a code word to confirm. That was it."

"That was Monday?"

She nodded.

He didn't remove his gaze from her. "And two days later he's dead."

She swallowed hard, lips compressing tightly together once more.

"You knew it was him," Buck said. "The minute we got word about the homicide."

She chose her answer carefully. "It seemed too much of a coincidence. I was afraid he'd been made. But I didn't have the authority to investigate and there was no evidence to suggest I should go over your head. I follow orders."

Buck leaned back in the squeaky leather chair, his expression impassive now, studying her. "One thing about working for me," he said, after a long time. "You'll find I'm the easiest guy in the world to get along with as long as you tell me the truth. But I can't have a man on the force who lies to me."

She stiffened. "Sir, I never lied."

"You lied about what you were doing here! You came in here pretending to work for me and your loyalties were never with this office!" A sharp breath, and his tone returned to even. "The men and women in this department are a team. More than that, we're a family. I've worked with some of them ten years. A lot of them didn't think it was a good idea to bring an outsider in. A lot of them didn't think you'd ever fit in. But I stood up for you. I told them to give you a chance. Now it turns out they were right. I don't think you even want to fit in here."

She flinched. "Sir, that's not true. I—I wanted to come here. I asked for this assignment."

His gaze narrowed sharply. "To spy on me?"

"No sir. To work for you."

"Then you should have worked for me. We would have gotten to the bottom of this a lot sooner if you hadn't been so damn worried about following orders and just told me what you knew."

She swallowed back a response. The response would have been, of course, that she had asked to be assigned to the case and he had told her it was out of their jurisdiction.

He answered what she did not say, his tone sharp. "You should have fought harder."

She said, "Yes sir."

She waited. He said nothing, just regarded her silently, rubbing his chin with his thumb and forefinger, thinking.

At last he said quietly, "We both need to spend some time thinking about whether you're a good match for this job. Meanwhile, get back to duty. The FBI will probably have some questions for you when they get here."

She stood up. "Yes sir." She hesitated. "Sir, do you think..." Her own brow puckered as she struggled with the question. "Could it have been because of me...my phone call...that got him killed?"

Buck's expression softened, but only fractionally. And all he could do was shake his head. "I don't know. You did what you were told. You didn't have a choice."

She nodded and turned to the door. He stopped her.

"You said Brunner had infiltrated a group of dissidents," he said, frowning. "What kind of dissidents?"

She replied, "Terrorists."

# CHAPTER TWELVE

Some people like to do; some people like to teach. I like both so much that if I were given a choice between crossing the finish line in record-breaking time with a clean run and watching a student do the exact same thing—well, I'm not sure which I'd choose. But I do know there can't be much in life that is more fun than seeing the big grin on a kid's face the first time he tells his dog to jump over a bar and he actually does it. Gosh, I love my job.

Of course, it wasn't all smiles and puppy kisses on the first day of class. There was the sheltie who took up residence in the tunnel and refused to come out. The goldendoodle who relieved himself on the dog walk. The Chihuahua who insisted on crawling under the six-inch jumps instead of leaping over them. When Monty, with her Great Pyrenees on leash, took off running and her dog did not, she took a tumble and scraped her knee. Willie was there in his ATV to transport her to the nurse within moments of my pressing the button on my radio, and she and her big dog rode off in style, looking more pleased with the attention than hurt.

Cisco, my faithful demo dog, was so excited by the abundance of fresh kids to pet him and fresh dogs to play with that he had a hard time focusing on his job. He had a tendency to take one jump and turn back to the crowd with a grin, waiting for applause, or to scramble through the tunnel and keep on going to the nearest child, mugging for a rubdown. That wasn't entirely okay, of course, but as I tried patiently to explain to my students, no dog is completely at his best on the first day in a new place. I hope that made some of the kids feel better about their dogs; I know it made me feel better about mine.

By the end of the class we had gotten the sheltie to leave the tunnel, everyone had completed the course, and most of the kids were eagerly looking forward to competing in our mock agility trial on Sunday. I went to lunch with a bounce in my step.

I had told Melanie I would meet her at 1:00 for our lake excursion, so I didn't linger at the instructors' table after I finished my meal. Willie Banks was pulling up in front of the dining hall when I came out, and I waved to him. He acknowledged me with a nod.

"How's Monty?" I called as I came down the steps.

He gave me a flat look under the brim of his straw hat in response, so I explained, "The little girl with the big dog who scraped her knee at the agility field."

He spat tobacco juice on the ground. "Yeah, she's okay I reckon. I left her at the nurse's office. That's all I'm supposed to do."

He started up the steps past me, and when we were abreast I said, "Say, Willie, have you noticed anybody up here doing target practice?"

He stopped and stared at me. Actually, it was more of a glare. "What're you talking about?"

"I found some shell casings and a straw target when I was setting up the agility equipment this morning."

He said, "Nobody's allowed up here unless they got permission. That's my job, to keep them out."

I shrugged and continued on my way. Clearly, he wasn't about to confess to anything that might indicate he hadn't been doing his job. "Just wondering if you saw who it was."

"I had to chase some fellas off a while back that wanted to play paintball," he said abruptly to my back. "And that's just what I did, too, you better believe it. Chased them off."

I gave him a casual smile over my shoulder. "Okay, thanks. See you later."

He did not smile back.

I stuffed some towels and floating toys into my knapsack and changed into my swimsuit, not because I was planning to swim, but because by the time four dogs finished shaking themselves dry, I would be as wet as they were. On the other hand, the noonday sun was so hot you could practically hear the grass crackle, and I was glad I wasn't holding a class that involved running and jumping in that big open field this time of day. Maybe a swim wouldn't be such a bad idea after all.

The path to the lake was not shaded, and the dogs were panting at the ends of their leashes as Melanie and I trotted behind. The sun baked my scalp and my shoulders, and I wished I had worn a tee shirt over my suit, instead of just a pair of shorts. Guiltily, I remembered my promise to Miles and demanded of Melanie, "Did you remember sunscreen?"

She replied easily, "Sure, I always remember. So as I was saying, this big Doberman comes rushing after the disc, but Pepper cuts in from the side, you know, and leaps six feet straight up…"

I doubted that but didn't say anything.

"…to snatch it right out of the air before it hit his face! She was amazing! Mr. Lee said she could go to competition level if she wanted to."

Once upon a time, I was ten years old and life was full of possibilities and all I had to do was choose between them. I said, "So what do you think?"

"I haven't decided yet," replied Melanie sensibly. "Pepper has lots of choices."

I agreed, "Good for you. Get all the offers before you sign to a team."

For a moment she looked uncertain, and then she grinned. "Right."

"Hey," I said. The lake was in view, twenty yards away. I knelt down and put my hand on Cisco's collar. His panting increased tempo. "Ready?"

Melanie nodded and knelt beside Pepper.

"Set...go!" I unclipped Cisco's leash, and then Mischief's and Magic's. Melanie released Pepper.

I wasn't worried about letting the dogs off leash this close to the lake. Pack behavior is fairly predictable, and I knew the other three would follow Cisco, whose gaze was so intent on the water that his eyes would probably get there before the rest of him did. Sure enough, as soon as I released his collar, Cisco took off at a leap. We laughed out loud as the pack scrambled down the remainder of the hill and followed Cisco as he dived—belly-flopped is more like it—into the water. The truth is, Mischief and Magic don't even like to swim, but they followed Cisco because, well, that's what dogs do. Even Pepper, who had only had swimming lessons at the doggie spa with its bone-shaped pool, plowed gamely into the fray, dog-paddling with the best of them.

Melanie waded knee deep into the water and tossed a floating ball for the dogs to retrieve. I snapped photos on my phone and e-mailed them to Miles. He responded with a text, "Wish I were there!" I sent back a smiley face, because I was in a very good mood. Seriously: a mountain lake, a summer day, happy dogs splashing in the water—who *wouldn't* be in a good mood?

I spread out a towel and sat down in the newly mowed grass, and as soon as I did Mischief and Magic scrambled out of the water and romped over, waiting until they had reached me to shake themselves all over me, just as I knew they would. I held up a hand in self-defense but too late. Actually, the cold water felt kind of good, and I was glad I'd worn my swimsuit. I dug another towel out of my knapsack and was drying them off when Melanie trotted up, Pepper at her heels. Pepper shook herself, spraying us both, and Melanie laughed. I wiped water off my face with the dog-hair covered towel, then tossed it to Melanie, who did the same.

"Leash," I reminded her.

"Pepper doesn't need a leash," she assured me. "She never leaves me."

"Yeah, well, do you want the first time to be in the middle of the Nantahala Forest?"

"Cisco would find her," she replied confidently, and just to be a show-off, tossed the ball across the grass. Pepper scampered after it.

It was at that moment that Cisco the Wonder Dog streaked out of the lake, paws spattering mud, coat shedding water. I grabbed for him but I never had a chance. He had his eye on something beyond my shoulder, and I turned in time to see him skid to a brief stop, snatch it up, and give it a shake. It was, I realized only later, the sock I had found last night and tossed away. Before I could even draw a breath for the command that I was almost certain would be ignored, Pepper galloped up with her ball in her mouth, teasing and play-bowing to him. The two of them engaged in one excited, high-speed round of catch-me-if-you-can, and then Pepper twirled and took off toward the woods, Cisco in hot pursuit.

Here's the thing about dogs. They are *dogs*. Not children with fur, not miniature humans, not mindless robots we can control. They are an entirely separate species, with a culture, language and agenda all their own. They may choose to share our lives with us, cooperate with us, and even, occasionally, obey us. But they are dogs, and the minute we forget that is the moment they will remind us they have minds, and wills, of their own.

Cisco never lets me forget that. I hoped, after today, Melanie would not forget it either.

She cried, "Pepper!" and started to lunge after her, but I caught her arm. Fortunately, after three years of living with Cisco's impulsive and all-too-often unpredictable behavior, my instincts have been honed to a razor-sharpness.

I commanded, "Mischief, Magic, down!" almost before their ears could even swivel in the direction of the runaways, and I snapped on their leashes as they dropped to their bellies. I handed Melanie the leashes, said, "Stay here. I'll get them." I looped Cisco's and Pepper's leashes around my neck and ran after Cisco just as his waving yellow tail disappeared into the bushes.

This was hardly my first time chasing my independent golden through the woods, although I will say I was glad that this time, at least, it wasn't entirely his fault. I knew it would be futile to call him when he was in hot pursuit of his current favorite playmate, so

I didn't even try. The part of a dog's brain that was created to chase prey is much older and more powerful than the part that recognizes human language, and when you put those two in conflict, the chances that it will turn out the way you want are not very good. So I didn't waste my breath. Cisco was a tracking dog—or to be more accurate, a tracking dog in training—and he could hardly be blamed for doing what came naturally to him. I could, however, blame myself for not insisting that Melanie leash Pepper, or leashing her myself, or grabbing Cisco the minute he got out of the water, for not calling him to me the minute he started for shore. And I cursed myself every sweaty, thorny, poison-ivy infested step of the way as I jogged after him into the woods.

Every time I came near enough to see him, Cisco had his nose to the ground, so he clearly was on Pepper's trail, which was a good thing. Of course, the moment he noticed me, he would be off at a gallop again, which was, in his mind, precisely what he was supposed to do. Now and then I caught a glimpse of two waving golden tails instead of just one, and I knew the game of chase was still on…only now the only one doing any chasing was me. The two of them persisted upon maintaining just enough of a lead to stay out of reach, which only proves their innate intelligence. If I could have caught either of them just then I doubt I'd be able to remember much about positive reinforcement dog training.

We seemed to be on a deer trail, and those usually led to water. Since I could hear the gurgling

of the stream that fed the lake, I knew we weren't
far away from trail's end. I also knew that the dogs'
romp would be over the minute they stopped to
play in the stream. I was right on both counts, but
I hadn't entirely expected what I found when I followed Cisco through a pine copse and into a narrow
clearing.

We had stumbled onto the site of a small camp.
There was a one-man tent, a fire pit encircled by
stones, a green bear bag suspended from a tree that
was devised to keep woodland creatures away from
good-smelling things like soap and food. It occurred
to me that this was probably the source of the sock
Cisco kept wanting to play with; the camper was
probably used to walking down to the lake to bathe
or do laundry. Pepper sniffed around the fire pit,
clearly worn out with the game and ready to call it
quits. But as I watched in horror, my agility dog, who
had been known to sail across a six-foot broad jump
without batting a lash, took a running leap into the
air and snagged the bottom of the bag with his teeth.
He looked as surprised as I was when the contents of
the bag came pouring down on his head.

His surprise lasted only a moment, though. He
dove into the bounty like a kid at a Christmas piñata,
followed quickly by Pepper, and by the time I stumbled forward to grab their collars and heave them
away, Cisco had consumed half the contents of the
bag.

"Cisco!" I cried, gasping. "Wrong!" I pried open
his mouth just to make sure there was nothing

dangerous inside—no remnants of plastic, no half-chewed deodorant bottles—then gave his collar a little shake. "Shame on you!"

If there is one phrase my dogs know without translation, it's *Shame on you*. Pepper didn't even need to know what it meant to understand my tone, and she stood contritely while I snapped on her leash. Cisco's ears dropped repentantly, but at the same time he licked the remainder of something delicious off his lips. It was an unconvincing apology.

I leashed Cisco and pulled both dogs close as I looked around in dismay at the remnants on the ground. The camper, whoever he was, had made an effort to preserve his provisions with waxed paper, but it had proven no deterrent to a determined golden retriever. And little wonder. The little packets of waxed paper, as far as I could tell, had contained strips of meat jerky, dried and smoked and absolutely irresistible to any dog. The average person might not believe that Cisco had tracked the scent of meat jerky all the way from the lake to the woods; the average person did not know my dog.

I spun at the sound of crashing through the woods, expecting the worst, but it was only Melanie. She had Mischief and Magic with her. On second thought, perhaps that was the worst.

"I told you to stay put!" I said, scolding.

"Pepper!" she cried, rushing forward with Mischief and Magic in tow and her face alight with relief. Pepper jumped up to greet her and I took the Aussie's leashes so she could hug her dog. "Pepper, you bad, bad, dog. I was so worried! Don't ever run away again!" She said it with such delighted adoration that Pepper had no idea she was being reprimanded and wriggled with pleasure as Melanie ruffled her ears and kissed her muzzle. Then she turned and grinned at me. "I told you Cisco could find her!"

Oh, to live in the world of a ten-year-old, where everything always, always turned out okay. I hardly knew where to begin with the lectures about how important it is to do as you're told, about how many things could have gone wrong, about how danger-ous it was to go tramping through the woods after a runaway dog—so I did not begin at all. I suspected she had already been scared enough when she saw Pepper disappear into the woods. Besides, I had more immediate problems.

"Here, take the dogs out of the way." Mischief and Magic were already starting to sniff the goodies on the ground, so I transferred their leashes back to Melanie. I did not trust her strength, however, to hold onto Cisco once he became focused on jerky, so I kept him by my side.

"I couldn't find Pepper's ball," she said, winding the leashes of all three dogs around her hand. "But Cisco dropped this." She thrust a dirty sock at me and then looked around the campsite. "Man, what a mess."

I stuffed the sock into my fanny pack, muttering, "You can say that again." I blew out a breath. "Well, the least I can do is try to clean up before the owner gets back."

"We should probably leave a note," Melanie agreed, "like when you have a fender-bender in the parking lot."

I wondered exactly how many fender-benders in parking lots she had had as I bent to start picking up scraps. Mischief and Magic resumed their curious sniffing and Pepper wasn't far behind. Cisco's leash was wearing a groove in my hand as he tried to stretch out his neck long enough that his tongue would reach the ground. "Dogs, sit!" I said sharply. The Aussies, looking not in the least put out, obeyed. Cisco followed more reluctantly. Pepper just stared at me.

Melanie said, "Pepper, sit," and Pepper obeyed.

I made a face that she couldn't see, but before I could comment, Cisco gave a short, staccato bark and lunged to his feet. Of course, that's all it took for the Aussies to break their sits, and Melanie wrestled with the three dogs. I reached to help her, but was stopped cold by an angry voice behind me.

"What the hell is going on here?"

I spun around, and found myself staring into the barrel of a shotgun.

# CHAPTER THIRTEEN

Special Agent L.J. Manahan was a tall, square man with silver hair and a firm handshake. He introduced his two colleagues, Lydia Armstrong and Jack Donaldson, as members of the Joint Terrorism Task Force. Nothing in any of their faces suggested they might be here to enjoy the Smoky Mountain scenery. Meeting them, Buck felt that bad feeling start to expand again.

The Hanover County Sheriff's Department had hosted an FBI task force before, less than a year ago. That time, they had been after one man—a hometown boy who'd made it to the Most Wanted list. A man Buck once had called friend. It had not ended well. Sometimes, late at night, Buck would lie awake staring at the ceiling, listening to the sound of those gunshots over and over again in his head.

Buck had not been in charge then. Now he was.

He said, "I think you'd better fill me in." He turned to lead the way to his office.

Manahan stopped him. "That's what we're here for, Sheriff. But first we need to set up a headquarters. We need a secure building with power and plumbing. We'll rewire what we have to. We have a van about twenty minutes behind us with more agents and equipment."

Buck cursed silently to himself, over and over again. No doubt about it now. This was bad. And it was on him. He said, "What about the old armory building on the edge of town? We've been using it as a kind of community center, but it's empty now."

Manahan nodded his head toward Jack Donaldson. "Check it out."

They were in the main bullpen, with everyone staring and trying to pretend they weren't, so it wasn't hard for Buck to get the attention of one of his men. He waved Lyle Reston over and said, "You and Mike take Agent Donaldson over to the armory and give him whatever assistance he needs." To Manahan, he said, "This way."

Once in his office, the female agent began unpacking her briefcase. An electronic tablet was hooked up to what appeared to be a miniature projector. In another moment a map of the southeastern United States appeared on the wall opposite. "You might recall that water treatment plant bombing in Alabama last year."

Buck nodded. "A little town called Bitter Branch, not much bigger than this. Crazy. You caught those guys, didn't you?"

"We caught two of them," said Manahan. "This"—a new overlay appeared on the map on the wall, with half a dozen red balloon-like symbols in

3-D appearing over the names of towns in Georgia, South Carolina, Louisiana, Tennessee and Mississippi that Buck had never heard of—"represents similar attempts in other small towns that we've been able to stop."

"Similar attempts," Buck repeated, staring at the map.

"They weren't all plots against municipal utilities," clarified Agent Armstrong. "The modus operandi vary. Sometimes facilities are targeted, sometimes individuals. On occasion multiple targets have been planned in the same location." She touched the screen of her tablet and a yellow arrow moved between a location in South Carolina and a location in southern Mississippi. "Here," she said, "a church was targeted. And here, a school."

The silence that descended upon the room was palpable for a brief moment, rich with both the horror of what might have happened and quiet pride that, in fact, it had not. Then Manahan said, "The goal appears to be to spread chaos. That's what terrorists do. And when they are successful, it doesn't matter how many of them we catch. They're like that snake with a thousand heads. You cut off one head and two grow in its place."

He nodded toward Armstrong, and another overlay appeared on the wall. It was blurred with red balloons, many of them so close together the geography itself was obscured. "These are the cells we suspect to exist, or to be in the process of forming, now. As you can see, the proliferation is primarily in the

Bible Belt, although we're seeing some significant activity in the Midwest as well. "

No one, looking at that map, could avoid feeling a little sick. Buck said softly, "My God. How do you fight them all?"

"One at a time," replied Manahan somberly.

Buck nodded slowly, beginning to understand. "And with explosives detection dogs from Homeland Security."

"Ideally, every law enforcement agency in the US would have at least one team like yours," said Manahan, "and eventually they will. For now, we're prioritizing according to strategic location and presumed threat. Your county met both those criteria. I'm not sure that's a good thing."

Buck muttered, "Me either." He looked sharply at Manahan. "I should have been briefed on what was going on. I can't be expected to do my job if I'm kept in the dark."

Manahan said, "We try not to involve local law enforcement until it becomes necessary. Most of the time, it's not necessary."

Agent Armstrong added, in a slightly less defensive tone, "We're making great strides in interagency cooperation, Sheriff. This task force is one example of that. Your Officer Smith is another. We're aware we have a way to go, but when we need to, we can still all work together to get the job done."

Buck couldn't think of a pithy reply to that, so he decided to go the route of cooperation. "Why small towns?" he asked. "Because they're easy targets?"

"Partially," agreed Agent Armstrong. "Partially because we think sentiment is already in their favor, and recruiting is easy."

Buck frowned. "I don't mean to tell you your business, but if there's one thing I can promise you it's that foreigners don't go unnoticed in a place like this. If a boy marries a girl from the next county it might take two generations before the neighbors stop looking at her sideways. I can tell you for sure that there is no way sentiment is in favor of terrorists around here."

Manahan returned mildly, "That would no doubt be true if we were talking about foreign nationals. These guys are as American as you and me. They call themselves Patriots, and they're building an army."

# CHAPTER FOURTEEN

Instinctively my arm shot out to shield Melanie, which might have been effective if we had been traveling sixty miles an hour in a car that came to a sudden stop. It was, needless to say, no barrier whatsoever against a twenty-gauge shotgun. Nonetheless, Melanie drew close to me.

"Raine," she whispered, big-eyed, "that's him. That's the man I saw yesterday at the lake."

He was thin and bearded, wearing jungle camo pants, worn hiking boots and a perspiration-stained gray tee shirt. His arms were covered with tattoos. He had the kind of droopy dark eyes that always remind me of Abraham Lincoln, except that Abraham Lincoln's eyes were kind. This man's eyes were hard and angry.

And then, when Melanie spoke, his eyes changed. It was as though he noticed her for the first time, and then the dogs, and he lowered the gun. My heart slowed to an almost normal rhythm, although his scowl was still far from reassuring. "What are you doing here?" he demanded fiercely. "Who are you?"

I stepped in front of Melanie, keeping Cisco close and slightly behind me. "I—I'm sorry," I said. "My dog got away from me. We were swimming down at the lake." My gesture was choppy and uncertain. "I'm really sorry…"

I looked around helplessly at the mess on the ground, and so did he. His expression changed again, from suspicion to dismay. He knelt on the ground, putting the gun beside his feet, and began to try to gather up the remainder of his provisions. The meat was covered with dirt and debris, slobbered on by dogs, and completely ruined. "You did this?" he said, and his voice sounded numb. He looked up at me with a fistful of meat strips in each hand and outrage in his eyes. "Why did you do this?"

I took an instinctive step backward, bringing Melanie and the dogs with me. "I didn't do it," I assured him quickly. "My dog did. He didn't mean any harm. I could pay you…" But even as I said it I wondered how I was going to pull that off, since the only thing I had in my back pocket was my cell phone. And I also knew something else: a man like this did not need money. Everything he needed was in that bag. And Cisco had destroyed it.

I finished weakly, "Is there anything I can do?"

He looked at Melanie, and at the dogs, and finally at me. He looked and sounded tired. "Just go home, lady. Just…go home."

"Maybe we could help you clean up…"

"Did you hear me?" His voice was sharp and I startled. "Just get the hell on out of here!"

I took Mischief's and Magic's leashes and said to Melanie with quiet urgency, "Let's go."

I walked so quickly back down the path that she had to trot to keep up with me, but I think she was more excited than scared as she demanded breathlessly, "Are you going to call the cops?"

We were by now well out of hearing range, and certainly out of sight, but still I didn't slow down. "No."

"Why not?" she demanded. Her eyes were big behind the glasses. "He had a gun!"

"Not everyone who has a gun is a bad guy," I told her. And because I noticed her face was red and sweaty even in the relative shade of the woods, and all the dogs were panting, I did slow down as the trail leveled out. "The first time I met your dad he had a gun," I added.

"Oh yeah?" She looked surprised.

"He was hunting behind my house," I explained. "People are allowed to hunt."

She scowled. "Well, I don't think they should be."

There was a part of me that privately agreed, but I also knew there were two sides to every story. "A lot of people around here feed their families by hunting." I thought of the man we had just left behind, and the dried strips of meat that were probably hand-smoked squirrel or possum. And probably all he would have to eat for the next month.

"My dad doesn't." She sounded angry and disappointed.

"That's true," I agreed. I let the dogs go to the end of their leashes, and now that the lake was in sight, I relaxed my shoulders a little. "But, whether we like it or not, these days Man is the only natural predator for a lot of species. Deer, for example. Without hunters to keep the population down, the herds would eat all the plants that other animals need to survive. Pretty soon there would be so many deer they couldn't even feed themselves and they'd starve to death too. It's called wildlife management, and even though it's hard to understand, it does help to keep nature in balance."

She was silent for a moment, and even though I knew the whole concept of natural selection and assisted husbandry was a bit advanced for a ten-year-old, I hoped at least I had done something to redeem her father in her eyes.

Melanie said, "I still think we should call the cops. He pointed a gun at us. You're not allowed to do that."

"No," I said. "That was stupid. But that doesn't make him a criminal. It just makes him an idiot. And my dad used to say that if you locked up every idiot there'd be nobody left to run the country."

A puzzled line appeared between her brows and I smiled, dropping a hand on her shoulder. "Look, the poor guy was just trying to enjoy the great outdoors when Cisco and Pepper came along and ruined his campsite and stole his dinner. If anyone's the bad guy, it's us."

She looked worried. "Is Cisco in trouble for tearing up the bag?"

I shook my head. "He was just being a dog. And you know it's pointless to punish a dog after he's already gotten away with the crime."

"So if the guy with the gun isn't in trouble, and Cisco isn't in trouble," she inquired reasonably, "who is?"

I sighed. "I am," I admitted unhappily, "for being the worst dog trainer ever." But then I managed a brief bracing smile and injected an upbeat note into my tone as I added, "And we're all going to be in trouble if we're late for our next class. So let's step on it, okay?"

# CHAPTER FIFTEEN

Buck said, "You're talking about a homegrown militia." But even as he spoke he was shaking his head. "Look, I'm not saying we don't have our share of good old boys talking a bad game, and that talk might get a little rowdy down at the Legion Hall on a Saturday night, but that's about as far as it goes. You're talking about the kind of people who'd put a bullet through a federal agent's head and then burn his body in a car."

"The FBI is aware that the vast majority of militia groups across the nation are mostly rhetoric," responded Agent Armstrong. "We have no interest in those. But the number of radical cells capable of plotting and committing violence against the government and its citizens has grown dramatically in the past eight years." She nodded again at the map. "And these we are very interested in."

"We think recruiting may begin with moderate militia groups, the kind you're talking about," Manahan said. "But then a selection process begins for the most radical, the most dedicated...misfits, mostly, usually ex-military. The cells are usually composed of members from a mixture of communities, which is why they're able to go undetected virtually under the noses of their friends and neighbors in small towns like these. They use their acts of terrorism to accelerate recruitment. Frightened people tend to take up arms and seek retaliation, particularly when they feel their own government can't protect them. The Alabama incident is a perfect example. It took those people months to put their community back together after the bombing."

"And four new radical cells formed within two hundred miles of the incident," said Armstrong.

"And you're telling me that one of these cells is operating right here, in my county."

"We believe so, yes."

Buck walked across the room to the small grimy window that looked out over the parking lot. He gazed at it for a moment, his hands in his pockets. Then he turned and looked at them. "What are we in for?"

Manahan didn't look happy. "Unfortunately, we weren't able to get much information from our agent before we lost him. We know there's an active cell here and we suspect they're planning something for this weekend."

"It fits the profile," put in Agent Armstrong. "These people like to take advantage of significant dates and events to stir public emotion."

"Like a popular congressional candidate making a speech on the Fourth of July?"

Manahan nodded tersely. "We've been in touch with Jeb Wilson's office, of course. But we've asked him not to publicly announce a change in schedule. The last thing we want to do is to let these people know we're on to them. In the past that's been known to accelerate the violence, not deter it."

Buck said, "Do you have any names?"

"Sheriff," said Manahan with chilling frankness, "we've got nothing but a dead agent and a credible threat."

"These cells are structured like military units," Agent Armstrong went on. "Each one has a commander, a second-in-command, foot soldiers who spend their weekends training and sentries to guard their resources and coordinate attacks. They use the Gadsden flag as their banner." Agent Armstrong flashed a picture of the Gadsden flag with its familiar rattlesnake and "don't tread on me" logo, just in case Buck didn't know what she was talking about. "What makes this movement particularly dangerous, and to be differentiated from similar ones over the years, is that all of the cells seem to be organized under a single leader, a general, if you will, who's coordinating all their movements. He's the one we're after, and up until now we thought we had a pretty good chance of closing in on him. That chance died with Carl Brunner."

Manahan said, "I presume you're running a full complement for the weekend? Extra security for the parade?"

Buck nodded. "The traffic doubles this time of year. My men have got all they can do to stay on top of the tourists and shoplifters."

Manahan nodded. "They should be briefed on what's going on, but otherwise proceed with their duties. The fewer people out there…" Buck knew he was about to say "getting in our way" but skipped that part and finished simply, "the better. Your K-9 unit should sweep the parade route Monday morning, but I imagine you'd already planned that."

Buck had not. But he hadn't known then what he knew now.

"As far as the public is concerned, the extra law enforcement presence is due to Jeb Wilson's appearance at the parade," Manahan went on. "From your end, it should be operations normal."

Buck said, "Operations normal. My pleasure. Meantime, I have a fellow you might want to talk to. His name is Reggie Conner, and I think I just figured out where he's been going when he told his daddy he was at AA meetings."

# CHAPTER SIXTEEN

Magic might have a lot of less-than-stellar qualities: she was a sneak thief, an escape artist unparalleled by anyone except her sister, and an unabashed chow hound. But she was an excellent obedience dog, she always came when she was called, and she never ran away without permission. She therefore won the honor of being my demo for obedience class that afternoon while Cisco rested in the cabin with Mischief. "Rested" was, of course, a generous word. If the truth were told, I wasn't feeling all that benevolent toward Cisco that afternoon and thought it was best if we took a break from each other.

The afternoon downpour came right on time, just as I began my obedience class. Eight squealing kids and barking dogs scurried for the rather frail shelter of our pop-up canopy. While rain drummed on our plasticized roof and the interior steamed with the smell of wet dogs and wet children, I improvised a quick lecture on the three qualities of a good leader, firmness, fairness and consistency, and I felt like a hypocrite. After all, if I practiced what I preached I wouldn't be the proud owner of a dog who took off like a wild hare after anything that struck his fancy, destroyed personal property and made me look like a fool.

After five minutes in which my human audience pretended to listen politely while struggling to keep their dogs from whining, barking, sniffing other dogs and chewing their leashes, I asked if there were any questions. A little girl whose paw-print lanyard ID tag read Matilda raised her hand. I acknowledged her gratefully. At least someone had been paying attention.

"Where did you get those earrings?" she asked. "They're really cute."

I had a feeling I was losing my audience, so I called Magic up and showed off her tricks—balancing a dog biscuit on her nose, jumping through my arms, playing dead—until the rain stopped a few minutes later. While the sun turned the swampy soccer field into a steam bath, I showed the children how each one of Magic's tricks had been based on an obedience behavior, and soon they were excited about teaching their dogs "sit," "come" and "down." I ended the class on a patriotic note, with all the dogs heeling happily around the ring while nibbling treats from their handlers' hands to the tune of "I'm a Yankee Doodle Dandy" playing from my portable boom box. All in all, not a bad save.

As soon as the kids scattered with their dogs for free time, I went to the camp store. I bought every package of beef jerky on display—there weren't that many, but some of the instructors liked to use them as training treats—along with packages of the dried fruit and trail mix that the parents had no doubt insisted we stock as snacks, and several bags of candy. From the kitchen I begged a package of hot dogs and some fresh apples. I offered to pay for them, but the cook just laughed and waved me off, replying that I wasn't the first person who had been in that day looking for hot dogs to use as training treats, and that Margie stocked extra for that purpose. The apples, she admitted, were a first, but they were free to all campers, and since they weren't exactly a fast-moving item, I was welcome to all I could use. I took her at her word and dumped a whole bowl into my sack.

I settled Mischief and Magic in the cabin with stuffed bones and promised them a long run after dinner. I filled Cisco's saddlebags with my purchases, strapped on his backpack and his leash and left for our hike. After all, I figured Cisco deserved a chance to redeem himself.

It took us a little longer than it had the first time, since I wasn't chasing a pair of golden retrievers going full-tilt through the brush. But the woods were cool and fragrant, the leaves still dripping rainwater and splashing my skin when I pushed aside branches, and I enjoyed the hike. As we approached the campsite, though, I put Cisco in a sit and commanded softly, "Speak."

He licked his lips, because he always likes to warm up for a performance, and barked once sharply. I called out, "Hello! We're friendly!"

I just wanted to introduce ourselves. The man had a gun, after all.

To be honest, there was a part of me that hoped he had moved on, and as we approached the campsite it looked at first as though that might be what had happened. There was nothing but the crunch of our footsteps as we approached the clearing; the campsite seemed deserted. But the tent was still up, the fire pit had not been covered. I looked around cautiously one more time but saw nothing.

"Okay, boy," I said softly, kneeling to unzip Cisco's saddlebags. "We tried, right? Let's do the deed and get out of here."

Like a wraith, he appeared from the shadows just beyond the campsite. "Just exactly what deed were you thinking about doing?" he demanded flatly.

I was relieved to see he was not holding a shotgun on me this time, but nothing else about his demeanor was reassuring. I swallowed hard, looking up at him. Cisco, sensing my distress, sat down.

"I, um, felt bad about what happened," I said, "so I brought some stuff. I know it won't make up for what you lost, but…"

As I spoke I hastily unpacked Cisco's saddlebags—packaged dried food, jerky, hot dogs—and placed the items on the ground like an offering. His expression went from fierce to puzzled, but when I started unpacking the apples, his eyes lit up. He bent and snatched the apple from my hand before I could place it on the ground, and bit into it with a muffled sound of pleasure.

"Man," he said in a moment, around a mouthful of fruit, "I haven't had apples in a coon's age."

I smiled and unpacked the rest of the fruit. Finally I took out a pillowcase and offered it to him. I didn't mind sleeping on a bare pillow; it was the least I could do. "It doesn't have a drawstring," I apologized, "but I've used pillowcases as bear bags before and maybe it'll do until you can replace the one Cisco tore."

He crunched on the apple, looking at the bounty spread before him, looking at Cisco, looking at me. I held my breath until he took the bag from me, swallowed, and said quietly, "That's right kind of you, ma'am."

I shrugged and got awkwardly to my feet. Cisco remained sitting, panting at the stranger in a beguiling fashion. "It seemed like the least we could do."

He stared at the provisions for a time. He took another bite of the apple, finishing it off, chewed and swallowed. He threw the core into the brush. He said, "Good to know there's still decent folks around, I guess."

Abruptly, he held out his hand to me. "Name's Gene Hicks. I'm sorry if I scared you and your little girl before."

I shook his hand, which was sticky with apple juice. "That's okay." I decided not to correct him about the relationship between Melanie and me. "I'm Raine, and this is Cisco."

He looked down at Cisco, and his long sad face seemed to ache with the faint smile it managed. He said, "Well now, you got him trained real good."

I said apologetically, "Not good enough, I'm afraid. I'm really sorry for what happened before."

Never one to miss an opportunity to press his advantage, Cisco got to his feet and wiggled over to the stranger, tail swishing, face grinning. The man bent over to pet him, ruffling his ears, massaging his jawline with his thumbs, the way Cisco liked. I relaxed by inches.

"Well now," he said, "I reckon you didn't know any better, did you, old fella? You look like a good dog to me, yes you do." I could see him begin to change as he ran his fingers through Cisco's thick golden coat, as he smiled into his eyes, as he clucked him under the chin. Dogs are magic. They always have been.

I said, noticing his accent, "Where're you from?"

"Florida, originally." He straightened up, and some of the defensiveness had left his eyes. "By way of everywhere."

"Are you hiking the Appalachian?" We weren't too far from the trail. "I started out the summer after high school but only got as far as Virginia."

He shook his head. "Nah. Just walking."

I sensed the shield come up over his face again as he knelt to start packing the food into the pillowcase. I reached into Cisco's backpack and took out the two bags of candy. "The one thing I craved on the trail was chocolate," I said, handing them to him. "And it's good for energy when, you know, you can't find anything else."

He took the candy from me without looking up, and he looked at it for a long time. Cisco waved his tail. I just stood there awkwardly.

In a moment he reached out and tugged Cisco's ear affectionately. He said, "I had a dog. Not like this one. A beagle. My little girl wanted a Snoopy dog." He let his hand drop and added, without looking at me, "Had to turn him into the pound when we lost our house. Couldn't afford the pet fee at the apartment, and another mouth to feed...well, it was hard. 'Bout broke my little one's heart. Mine too."

I felt something clench in my own chest. It was an all too familiar story in these economic times and it killed me, every single time, to see the desperate lengths to which people had been driven when they were forced to choose between a family member and...their family.

He thrust the candy into the pillowcase and went on, "Everybody was hard hit back home. First the economy went belly-up, then the damn oil spill in the Gulf, then it seemed like one hurricane right after another...but that's okay, right? Everybody's got insurance, right? The government going to take care of what wasn't your fault, right?"

It seemed to me he was almost throwing things in the pillowcase now, and there was no mistaking the bitterness in his voice. "And wouldn't you know it—the only thing I knew how to do was build houses. I was good at it too. Had a nice house of my own, a couple of spec-builts on the market, two cars, twelve men working for me. Paid my taxes on time, went to church, listened to all the right people—the banker that told me to put my savings in stocks, the insurance man that said I was covered, the government that told me we had the strongest economy in the world. And even when everything went south, I believed them when they said things were going to turn around, I did my best to keep the payroll going, I believed them when they told me the safest place for my money was still right where it was." He gave a small grunt of contempt. "If I'd've kept that money under my pillow all those years, I might've saved my house."

"Anyway." He sat back on his heels. "We lost everything inside of two years. We were able to hold onto one of the spec houses and live on the rent plus whatever odd jobs I could pick up, until the storm came. The tenants were okay, thank the Lord, but the house was leveled. Sticks. And do you know how much the insurance paid on it? Three hundred dollars." He shook his head slowly. "All those years, never missed a payment. Three hundred dollars."

I said uncertainly, "I don't understand. How can they do that?"

He shrugged. "I don't understand it either. They said my claim was being pursued. That was three years ago. After a while, you get so beaten down you just can't fight anymore, and I guess that's what they're counting on. Anyway, you might say that was the last straw. My wife just kind of fell apart after that, piece by piece. So did I, I reckon. We tried to put the pieces back together but there were just too many missing. My little girl, she had asthma, you know, and her medicine was so expensive… Here's my tax money bailing out the fat cats on Wall Street that got us into this mess in the first place, and we're living on food stamps and odd jobs and can't afford insurance to pay for my little girl's asthma. Ah, hell, we didn't have a chance.

"After a while the wife went to live with her sister in Des Moines and took my baby with her. There was nothing I could do for them. I couldn't stop her from trying to make a better life for herself, for my little girl. Me, I just started walking. Looking for something, I don't know what. It's not such a bad life, on the road. And I guess at least if you're wearing out shoe leather, you're doing something."

The afternoon seemed still and heavy. The birds weren't chirping, the squirrels weren't scurrying, even the rain had stopped dripping from the leaves. Cisco, stretching out his paws, lowered himself to the ground and lay down, quietly. Gene Hicks watched him. He kept on watching him even as he spoke again, at last, in a strained and stifled voice. "You know the thing I regret the most?" he said. "The one thing I wish I could change? I wish I could have found a way to keep that damn dog." He reached out once more and stroked Cisco's chin. "She sure was crazy about that animal."

He stood up. "Anyway, I thank you kindly for this." He lifted the bulging pillowcase in acknowledgement. "And I don't hold no grudge against your dog."

I nodded. My throat was too thick, and my eyes too hot, to speak for a moment. I tugged on the leash and Cisco got to his feet. Gene walked over to the tent and pushed back the flap to place the provisions inside. I caught a glimpse of a neatly rolled sleeping bag, a green cotton backpack and a couple of small cardboard boxes near the entrance. As he swung the bag inside, he dislodged one of those boxes, spilling the contents out onto the ground. Cisco was quick to investigate, and before I could stop him had shoved his nose into a box and had come up with something else he shouldn't have.

"Whoa, there, old boy," said Gene, reaching for his collar.

At the same time, I cried, "Cisco, drop it!"

Cisco knew when he had pushed his luck and he relinquished his bounty with absolutely no prompting into Gene's waiting hand.

"Firecrackers," explained Gene, hastily returning the big fused cylinders to the box. "I was going to try to sell them in town." He smiled a little. "Maybe I'll set off a few for the kids tonight. Happy damn Fourth of July, right?"

I tried to return the smile, although I couldn't stop thinking about my dog who'd just tried to bite through an explosive. "Right," I said, and turned to go.

"They say when you go through bad times," he said, "you're supposed to learn something. What I learned was you can't trust anybody: not the government, not the banker, not the preacher. Not your wife. Not anybody. You might ought to keep that in mind."

I turned to look at him, a little chilled. His Abraham Lincoln eyes took on an even more somber hue. "You take care of that little girl, you hear? There's some bad types around."

I nodded. I cleared my throat and managed, "You can stay here as long as you want, you know. You're on public land."

"I know." He inclined his toward the lake. "Some good fishing down there too. But I'll wait till you all move out to try it again."

I tried to smile. It wasn't a very valiant effort. "Well," I said, "it was nice meeting you."

He did not reply, and Cisco and I walked back down the trail in silence. It wasn't until I was all the way back at the camp that I realized I had forgotten to return his sock.

# CHAPTER SEVENTEEN

The Hanover County Sheriff's Department ran two twelve-hour shifts. Buck waited until the seven p.m. watch change to brief both shifts. They didn't have an official meeting room big enough to accommodate the whole department, so he sat on the edge of one of the desks in the bullpen while everyone else pulled up desk chairs or stood around the edges of the room. They had all heard rumors, and were anxious to have them confirmed.

"Good news, guys," Buck said. "We finally got some help from the FBI controlling these damn tourists."

A few chuckles went around the room, partly polite, mostly nervous. Buck's gaze went from man to man, catching as many eyes as he could, resting just long enough on Wyn to acknowledge her slight, almost imperceptible nod of encouragement.

He said, "Here's the deal. Seems like we've got a few bad-asses out there who like to dress up as soldiers and plant bombs to make their point. What the hell their point might be is anybody's guess and I for one don't care. The FBI thinks Jeb Wilson might be their next target. Our job is to make sure it isn't. I hope by now you've caught on to the fact that we're damn lucky to be one of the few counties in western North Carolina to have a K-9 team with a specialty in bomb detection so let's give Deputy Smith and Deputy Nike some respect, am I right?"

A round of cheers, led by Wyn, went around the room, along with some hearty applause that was mostly designed to break the tension. Jolene, who sat in one of the desk chairs with Nike at her feet, remained straight-shouldered and impassive. And anyone who bothered to notice would have seen that there was very little warmth in Buck's eyes when he looked at her.

He went on, "As far as the FBI is concerned, we're here to guard the borders, and that suits me fine. Operations normal. But just in case you should happen to stumble on to one of these assholes in the course of normal operations, here's what you're looking for."

He gave them a condensed version of what he had learned from Manahan, and then stood up to pass a handful of flyers to the man on the front row, who took one and passed them on. "We're also interested in speaking with one Reggie Conner in connection with the death of Carl Brunner. He is not, repeat, not, a suspect in this case, merely a person of very particular interest who seems to have better things to do than make himself available for an interview. Maybe he's got an important barbecue to attend, maybe he's out at a ball game, maybe he's taking advantage of our beautiful Smoky Mountain wilderness on this fine holiday weekend, but he's starting to piss me off. If you happen to run into him, do not apprehend, but call the number on your poster there. Wyn and Les, I want you in the lead on this."

Wyn nodded. Buck went around the room, confirming weekend assignments, and ended with, "Deputies Smith and Nike, you're on PR duty, as previously assigned. Report in for your regular shift Monday morning to do a sweep of the parade route and consider yourselves on high alert until otherwise notified. Dismissed, everybody, and have a safe shift."

Jolene waited until the room had emptied to come up to her boss, Nike at an automatic heel. She said, "Sir, I think I could be more helpful if I took an active part in this case."

He said, gathering up his papers, "You have your assignment."

"That was humiliating!" Her eyes flashed. "We're in the middle of a crisis and you practically gave me the weekend off! You're sending me to a kids' camp when there's a terrorist threat. That's what I'm trained for. Let me do my job!"

Buck's expression was controlled, his tone only slightly gentled with compassion. "I finally got around to reading your record," he said. "I think we're all better off if you stick to your assignment."

Something went out of her, a little color, a little courage. But still she insisted. "You told me I should have fought harder. I'm fighting for this. Sir, I need to do my job."

"Then do it," he said shortly. "Your assignment stands." He turned for the door, and then looked back. For a moment there was a hint of something very close to debate in his eyes, but then he said, "I need people by my side that I can trust. I'm sorry. You're not one of them." And he left.

Only a very select number of people had the private number of the Professor. When he saw the caller ID, he answered immediately.

"The FBI has set up a task force," the voice on the other end said. "They know about Brunner. They haven't identified anyone else. They're expecting activity on the Fourth, with Wilson as the target. The bomb dog will sweep the area Monday morning."

"Excellent," said the Professor. His voice was calm, completely in control. "Operation Independence begins at oh-two hundred this day. Acknowledge."

"Acknowledged." There might have been a slight quickening of breath, a tightening of voice. A simple enough homage to the historic scope of this moment.

The Professor said, "This is what we've worked for, waited for, prepared for. We are equal to it. 'Let every nation know, whether it wishes us well or ill, that we shall pay any price, bear any burden, meet any hardship, support any friend, oppose any foe to assure the survival and the success of liberty.' Do you know who said that, by chance?"

There was a hesitation. "No, sir."

"I didn't think so." His voice was a mixture of compassion and amusement. Then briskly, "Good work, Deputy. I shall see you on the field of battle."

"Yes, sir."

The Professor disconnected the call and muttered, "It was John Fitzgerald Kennedy, you idiot."

He turned and took the steps of the building two at a time. He was late for a meeting.

# CHAPTER EIGHTEEN

After the episode with Gene Hicks, it was kind of hard to get back into my usual cheerful mood. I took Mischief and Magic for the promised run, and since Cisco seemed to have learned his lesson, I allowed him to come along too—although on leash. We angled away from the lake this time, along one of the old bridle trails, but hadn't even gone a quarter of a mile before I heard engine sounds. I barely got leashes on Mischief and Magic and pulled them off to the side of the road before a jeep came barreling around the corner, blowing up dust and completely oblivious to whatever might be in his path. The driver might have been Reggie, the guy with the weed eater we'd met yesterday, but he didn't acknowledge me and I couldn't be sure.

It was a close call, and the run was ruined for me, so we headed back to camp and caught the last part of the Canine Idol auditions. Pepper won a spot for her Counting trick, in which she would bark out the number of dog biscuits Melanie held up. The real trick, of course, was that Melanie would reward her with a biscuit before she exceeded the correct number of barks, but I still thought it was clever. Apparently so did the judges, Margie and Steve, and Melanie was grinning from ear to ear when she received her competitors badge for the show.

"Of course," she told me seriously as we walked back to the doggie dorm so that she could feed Pepper, "I'm not sure if we're going to have time to work on a whole routine for the show. Pepper's got a part in the play on Saturday night, and she has to learn her lines. And I don't want her to be too tired to win the agility trial Sunday morning."

I fought back a grin. "Sometimes you just have to prioritize," I agreed. "But it's good to have options."

But even saying that made me sad again, because it reminded me of the guy in the woods whose options had all be been taken away.

Melanie went on brightly, "We learned the Big Finale for the play today. Do you want to hear it?" And without regard for whether I did or not, she began to sing to the tune of "America the Beautiful":

*Oh, beautiful for collie dogs*
*And German shepherds too,*
*For poodles and Siberians*
*With shining eyes of blue!*
*Oh Labradors, oh Rottweilers,*
*Oh spaniels all springy*
*Throughout the days*
*We sing your praise*
*You're everything to me!*

I laughed all the way back to my cabin.

I sat on the porch of my cabin and called Miles while the dogs were inside scarfing down their dinner, and before I knew it I was telling him about the whole incident with the runaway dog, the demolished bear bag, the homeless camper.

"Let me get this straight," he said when I had finished. His voice had that deliberately calm tone it often took when he wasn't particularly calm at all. "You went back out into the woods, alone, to find an angry man with a gun."

I scowled uncomfortably. "I wasn't alone. Cisco was with me."

"When is Parents' Day? It sounds like I need to come get you."

"Oh, for heaven's sake. You're completely missing the point."

"The part about the gun?"

"The poor guy lost everything, Miles. I just feel so bad for him."

He was silent for a moment. "I do too, sweetheart. Unfortunately, it's not an uncommon story. Everybody was hurt by the recession, including myself. There are far too many men like him out there, and a lot of them are angry. They have a right to be. But I just wish you would stay away from this one, okay?"

I bit down on what I was thinking, that he might think he had been hurt by the recession, but there was a big difference between having to postpone buying a new jet because of the economy, and having to turn your dog into the pound because you couldn't afford to feed him. Miles was definitely on the wrong side of this story.

Then he redeemed himself by adding, "Honey, I'm sorry this guy ruined your weekend. I know how much you were looking forward to it."

"He didn't ruin the weekend," I said. "It's just that…oh, Miles, do you ever wish you could be a kid again?"

"Yeah, baby," he admitted with a sigh. "I do. Even though my childhood wasn't exactly out of a storybook, I'd trade it for being grown up in a heartbeat."

I settled back on the step, leaning my weight on one elbow, watching a cardinal hop from one branch to another in the maple tree across the path. "Did you go to camp?"

"Nah, we didn't have the money. I used to spend my summers at the Y, playing basketball, swimming, putting cherry bombs in toilets, that sort of thing."

I choked on a surprised laugh. "You were a bad boy!"

"Sweetie, you don't know the half of it. One year my buds and I got hold of some M-80s and almost blew out the side of the damn building. We'd've ended up in jail if anyone found out, but I guess the statute of limitations has run out by now."

"Oh, well. I guess I won't bother turning you in then."

"I appreciate that. I'd also appreciate you not ratting me out to my daughter. I'm trying to set an example."

I chuckled. "Speaking of Parents' Day, Pepper's going to be in the talent show Sunday. Be sure to make a big fuss when Melanie tells you about it."

"You bet I will. What time does the show start?"

"Be here at two," I told him. "They're having refreshments for the parents and a tour of the camp before the awards are given out, and the talent show is the last thing."

He said, "Can't wait." And the thing is, I knew he meant it.

"Umm, also," I added, "you might be in for a lecture about deer hunting. The subject came up. Just a heads-up."

In the silence that followed, I could hear Cisco pushing his metal bowl across the floor inside, always a sign that he was looking for more. The Aussies' dinner would be in jeopardy if I was not there to supervise, so I stood and went to the door, glaring sternly at Cisco. He watched me out of the corner of his eye, pretending innocence.

Miles said, "Didn't I hear somewhere you had a degree in wildlife science? You couldn't have diffused the subject?"

I shrugged. "Hey, I'm on the deer's side."

"Have I mentioned lately how glad I am I met you?"

I grinned to myself. Like I said, Miles always finds a way to make me laugh. "Gotta go," I said. "Twenty-five miniature campers and all that."

He said, "Love you, babe. Have a good night."

Here's the difference between Miles and me. He tossed his love around like confetti at a parade: he loved my dogs, he loved Melanie, he loved apple pie. He loved me. I hoarded my love like a fragile crystal I was afraid would get broken if I allowed anyone to touch it. I wished I could be as open and easy with my feelings as Miles was, but I couldn't. He never let on that it bothered him, and maybe it didn't. But it bothered me.

"You, too." It was all I could manage, but I said it with tenderness, and he knew what I meant.

At least, that's what I wanted to believe.

It is virtually impossible to be in a bad mood while sitting around a campfire singing camp songs like "How Much is that Doggie in the Window" and "Bingo" while melting chocolate and marshmallows between two graham crackers—not to mention trying to keep twenty-five dogs of all sizes and energy levels safe and happy. All of the instructors and counselors earned their money that night, and there were times that I laughed until my face hurt. Afterwards, the instructors all walked back to the cabins together while the counselors got the kids settled in their dorms for the night. We lingered on the porch of Margie and Steve's cabin, chatting informally about the kids and how we thought things were going, about the plans for tomorrow and the facility in general. Cisco, Mischief and Magic who, with the exception of a few stolen marshmallows, had been model citizens at the campfire, sniffed around at the ends of their leashes, occasionally sidling up hopefully to one of the instructors, remembering that they always carried treats.

"I think I'm going to talk to the owners about booking it again for next year," Margie said. "It might be a little run-down, but it really is perfect for what we need. All the different covered pavilions, the fenced fields, and that Girl Scout camp in Tennessee has gotten to be so unreliable. They refuse to book a year in advance, and you see what happened this time…"

I was standing on the next to the bottom step when the explosion cracked the air. I whirled and almost fell off the step, saved only by Cisco, who jumped up with his paws on my chest and pushed me against the railing. Before I could right myself, there was another explosion and another. Dogs started barking.

"Oh, look!" Margie exclaimed, pointing toward a shower of red sparks that were dissipating against the night sky. There was another cracking boom, and an umbrella of gold spread across the sky.

"Somebody's celebrating early," commented Lee, pushing himself to his feet. "Guess I'd better check on the thunder-phobic dogs."

I rubbed Cisco's shoulders to disguise my own frazzled nerves. He panted anxiously in my face. He wasn't exactly thunder-phobic, but he wasn't wild about fireworks. Or gunshots. "Do you need any help?" I asked.

"Nah. You've got your own crew to worry about. But say, how about letting me borrow one of your Aussies tomorrow for the flying disc class?" He had brought his own dog, an Irish terrier who knew more tricks than any dog I'd ever met and had actually starred in a couple of television commercials, but who could care less about chasing things that flew.

I assured him that would be no problem at all just as another fireball exploded in the distance. I took Cisco's paws and lowered them to the ground, untangling his leash from Mischief's and Magic's.

"Honestly," Margie sighed. "Why can't they wait until Monday?"

"Some people just have more to celebrate than others, I guess," her husband replied. "I'll give Lee a hand."

I said good-night and walked next door to my cabin, and the last starburst fizzled overhead as I climbed the steps.

Happy Fourth of July. I guess.

# CHAPTER NINETEEN

Saturday started off beautifully, with another sunrise run around the camp—this one blissfully uninterrupted—followed by a six-thirty staff meeting over banana pancakes.

"This is my favorite day of camp," Margie declared, pressing her hands together and grinning like a kid herself. "Dog demo day! The kids get a chance to see how they can take what their dogs have learned so far to the next level, and of course we always like to use as many of our campers as we can in the actual demonstrations. For everyone's peace of mind, of course, the camper dogs will be crated in the dorm during the demos. I believe Counselor Haley has the duty today."

Haley, with blond braids and a mouthful of pancakes, lifted her hand good-naturedly.

"We have a full morning of classes, and right after lunch we'll start arts and crafts in the rec hall to give the rest of you time to set up for your demos. Our police dog team will be here at two, and the deputy will need some help setting up materials for her bomb-detection demo. I thought the north field would be a good place since the agility course is already set up and it would be great for the kids to see how a game like agility can be used to teach police dogs."

Counselor Bill looked mildly alarmed. "Excuse me, did you say bombs? They're bringing bombs here?"

Margie smiled and shook her head. "I've never actually seen a demo but I don't think they use real bombs."

As it happened, Melanie had sent me a link to an article not long ago on how bomb dogs are trained, because at that time she wasn't sure whether her future lay in training drug dogs for the DEA or bomb dogs for the private sector. The information was still fresh in my mind so I supplied, "It's the components of explosives the dogs are trained to smell. They don't actually have to be mixed together into a bomb in order to be detected. They can smell gunpowder on a policeman's hands, for example, even if he hasn't fired his weapon for hours, which is how you can get a lot of false positives when the dogs do demos at police academies."

There were some nervous chuckles, and I turned to Margie. "And that's why I don't think the agility field would be the best place for the demo. I found an old target and shell casings there when I was setting up yesterday. I think somebody's been target shooting while the camp was empty. It might distract the dog."

She looked disappointed. "I don't like to keep moving the kids from one arena to the other. It's so hard to keep them organized."

I thought about it for a minute. "Well, the grass is all mowed around the lake. If everything else is taking place up here, maybe we could do the search and rescue and police dog demos last and just have the kids walk down the hill. It would be a lot better for both demos if we had a clean field anyway, and you can get Willie to bring down the equipment we need on the ATV."

"That might work," Margie agreed thoughtfully. "We could still close with the parade of breeds—the kids are making some cute glitzy bandannas for their dogs to wear—here in front of the lodge."

"Be sure to announce play rehearsal at five thirty," Lee added. "It'll only take about twenty minutes, but if they want to be in the play tonight they need to be on time."

And on that note, Margie dismissed us all to begin our busy days.

Canine Nosework was my last class before lunch, and as the kids fanned out with their dogs toward the dining hall and the exercise areas, I let Cisco earn his keep by retrieving each of the stuffed toys I'd used for the lesson and placing them in my duffel bag. Actually, I was waiting for Willie, who was supposed to load up the tunnel and the miniature A-frame and take them down to the lake after I finished my morning agility class, which had been two hours ago. I had tried him on the radio earlier, but had gotten no response and figured he was out of range. I was about to try him again when the radio crackled in my hand.

"Raine, are you on your way in?" It was Margie.

"Five minutes. Have you seen Willie?"

"He's here somewhere. Our police dog has arrived."

I spared time for an incredulous face that no one could see before pressing the talk button. "She's early."

"We may have to rearrange the schedule a tad." Margie hated rearranging schedules. She was trying hard to sound cheerful. "Can you show her where you're going to set up?"

I picked up the duffel bag and Cisco's leash. "Do you mean after lunch?"

A hesitation. "I think she's in a hurry."

Well, bully for her. What did she think this was, on-demand theater and she was the star attraction? Is this what you do when you're a fancy-pants canine handler with a superhero dog, you just waltz into a camp full of kids and demand everything be rearranged to suit your schedule? Maybe when she was invited to dinner she arrived two hours early and demanded to be served so that she could get on with her day. Seriously, of all the nerve.

I pushed the Talk button. "On my way."

Cisco and I took our time, stopping by my cabin to drop off the duffle bag and to let Magic out of her crate. Mischief was working as demo dog with Lee in the flying disc class, and I'd agreed to pick her up at the rec hall after lunch. Since there wasn't a lot of damage Magic could do in such a small space before I got back, I left her loose in the cabin with a few chew toys and a bowl of water—first making sure all edibles were behind lock and key. Cisco and I sauntered back up the hill toward the main lodge, where I could see Jolene waiting impatiently beside the black K-9 unit SUV. Margie was with her, trying to look pleasant while keeping the children who wanted a sneak peek at a real police dog moving toward the dining hall. I felt a little sorry for her, and picked up the pace. Margie definitely looked relieved as she saw me approach.

"Well now, there she is," she said, a little too brightly. "Deputy Smith, I'll let Raine take over. You know each other, right? Raine, the deputy has to get back to work, so we're going to switch things around a little. We'll start the demos at the lake right after lunch, then move back up to the lodge for arts and crafts. That should work out, don't you think?" Without giving me a chance to reply, she added, "I'll make the announcement at lunch. It was a pleasure to meet you, Deputy, and thank you again for coming out."

She hurried away, but not before giving me a meaningful look that included a "Good Luck" eye roll toward the straight-shouldered deputy.

I said, "We weren't expecting you until two."

She looked annoyed at having to explain herself. "We had to make some changes."

"Good thing we're flexible."

Cisco, who had never met a stranger, wiggled and wagged his way over to her in greeting. She glanced down at him but made no overture, just let him stand there wagging his tail and grinning up at her. That annoyed me even more than her refusal to respond to my comment.

I said, "Cisco, with me." Disappointed, he came back over to me, sniffed my fanny pack for a possible treat, then wandered around to the end of the leash, exploring the gravel drive, occasionally looking up with his winning smile at the sound of a child's voice, just in case someone wanted to pet him.

I said, with all the false pleasantness I could muster, "Usually when Buck gives these assignments they come with the rest of the day off. You probably have plans you're in a hurry to get to."

She said coolly, "It's a holiday weekend, Miss Stockton. No one gets a day off. Now if you'll show me where I should set up…"

I turned at the sound of the ATV engine and lifted my arm to Willie, waving him over. He didn't respond, so when he pulled in front of the lodge and cut the engine, I cupped my hands around my mouth and called, "Willie, over here! We need your help!"

I turned back to Jolene. "We're going to do the police dog demo and the tracking demo down at the lake. Willie will take the equipment down in the ATV. Of course," I added with only the smallest smirk, "we'll have to do the tracking demo first, or the trail will be wrecked."

She frowned. "Can't you do that somewhere else?"

Before I could answer, Melanie jogged up, her face flushed from running and her eyes bright with excitement. "Hey, Raine," she said, "are you getting ready to show the police dog around? I can help you set up. Pepper's all exercised and in her crate."

As she spoke she gave Jolene the once-over and announced, "I'm going to train drug dogs for the FBI when I grow up."

Jolene glanced at her briefly. "Good for you."

"Are there a lot of dogs working for the FBI?" Melanie persisted. "Are their handlers men or women?"

"I wouldn't know," replied Jolene, and her attitude immediately aroused my protective instinct.

I said, "Melanie, you should go to lunch. We can't start the demos until everyone finishes."

"I can skip lunch," Melanie assured me. "They always have snacks for later. And I'd rather help you set up."

I said, "When I was at camp, I always used to hate the girl who got all the special attention. That's why I promised your dad you wouldn't get any. Go to lunch."

She turned back to Jolene. "Is Nike in the car? Raine said that was her name. Why don't you let her out? The other dogs won't bother her. They have to be in their crates at lunch."

Jolene looked meaningfully at Cisco, and that just made me side with Melanie. "It'll take half an hour to set up," I pointed out. "You shouldn't leave her in the car while we're gone."

She slid another one of those mildly contemptuous looks my way. "K-9s always stay with the unit," she responded. "It's their job."

"With all these curious children around?" I lifted a skeptical eyebrow. "We might have liability issues."

This was clearly a subject upon which she had not been fully briefed, and for the first time a shadow of uncertainty crossed her eyes. She said shortly, "Control your dog." She went around the vehicle to open the door.

I replied, "Cisco is always under control." But just to make sure, I added in a slightly lower tone to Cisco, "Cisco, down." He looked up to make sure I was serious, then stretched out at my feet. To Melanie I added, sotto voce, "Whatever you do, don't pet her dog."

She gave me a small eye roll. "I know that."

I glanced around and saw all but a few stragglers had already gone into lunch. "You get to look at her, that's all. No more questions. Or," I added over the objection I could see forming, "I'll find someone else to be the lost person in Cisco's demo."

I could see her debating, and for a moment I actually thought I might lose. Then, reluctantly, she nodded assent. "Okay."

Willie came up beside me. "What do you need?"

He looked tired and sweaty and a little out of sorts, which made me reluctant to ask him for a favor until I remembered that was what he was here for. "Hi, Willie. Looks like you had a busy morning."

He took off his straw hat and wiped his shiny forehead with the back of his arm. "That's right."

"Well, I hate to ask, but we've had to move the police dog demo up to first thing after lunch. The deputy has some equipment she needs you to take down to the lake, and we'll also need the tunnel and the A-frame from the agility field."

He frowned. "I'll have to make two trips. Get the pickup for the big stuff."

"I'm sorry."

Cisco made a soft greeting sound in his throat— not quite a whine and certainly not a bark, but he was definitely anxious to be released from his down. I tightened my hand on the leash and returned a warning, "Ank!" to him. He licked his lips and stopped whining, but his ears perked and his eyes shone alertly as he gazed in the direction of the K-9 unit. I looked up just as Jolene came around the vehicle with Nike on a heavy leather leash which I knew from experience she did not need.

I said to Jolene, "If you'll show Willie what you need for the demo, he can start loading it into the ATV."

Nike started sniffing the ground and Cisco grew agitated as she drew closer. I wound another loop of his leash around my hand and said soothingly, "Easy…"

It was at that moment that Nike positioned herself in front of me, sat and barked.

I knew an alert when I saw it; that was precisely what Cisco had been trained to do when he made a find. But why was she alerting on *me?*

Jolene frowned sharply at me. "Is this some kind of joke?"

Given the animosity between us, I could see why she might think that. Now that Nike was practically stepping on my toes, Cisco was panting so hard with excitement that he was almost wheezing, and I resisted the urge to move away from both the angry woman in uniform and the determined dog who, if I recalled, was not only trained to detect munitions but drugs. As far as I knew I was carrying neither, but…

"Holy cow!" Melanie exclaimed with sudden, delighted enlightenment. "She *is* good!" She looked at me excitedly. "Your fanny pack, Raine! Remember you put the bullets there?"

Jolene's gaze darkened with suspicion. "What's she talking about?"

"Reward your dog," I said, disguising my relief as I unzipped my pouch. "She's right."

Jolene reached for the knotted rope on her utility belt and tossed it to Nike, who jumped up in the air and snatched it like a puppy. Cisco almost lost his cool then, and I couldn't blame him. Nonetheless, I gave him a brief "Ank!" as a reminder and dug out the shell casing from the bottom of my pack.

"We found a bunch of these yesterday," I said, showing it to Jolene. "I saved one to try to find out what kind it was." Then I frowned. "Can she really smell a spent shell that's been lying around on the ground for weeks?"

Jolene took the shell from me. "It's an AR-15 round," she said.

Melanie's eyes grew big. "Like a machine gun?"

"Assault rifle," I corrected her. And then I thought, *Assault rifle? Here?* As anyone with television, radio or newspaper access knows, it's possible to legally purchase certain kinds of assault weapons in many states, North Carolina being one of them. You do occasionally see them at firing ranges, although what their owners were expecting to need them for was anybody's guess. Attack of the killer deer? Assault by deadly jackrabbit? Besides, the nearest rifle range was a good fifteen miles from here.

Jolene must've been thinking much the same thing because her frown deepened and her voice was tight as her hand closed around the shell. "Where did you find this?"

"We can show you," Melanie volunteered quickly.

But I gave her a stern look. "*I* can show her," I corrected. I could see a stormy argument forming in her eyes so I passed her Cisco's leash. "Do me a favor, take Cisco to the doggie dorm and put him in one of the spare crates, will you?" It wasn't that I didn't trust my guy around Nike, but he *was* awfully interested in her, and Jolene didn't seem to have a sense of humor about things like that. Besides, everything always went a lot faster without Cisco along, and the sooner we got this over with, the sooner I could get my lunch.

"But he hates being crated!" Melanie protested, pouting.

"Then put him in an ex-pen. I'll only be a few minutes. You can put Pepper in with him if you want."

That seemed to sweeten the deal somewhat, and I could see her relenting. I decided to push my luck. "And save me a sandwich from lunch."

She brightened. "I'll bring it to you at the lake! Come on, Cisco." And before I could correct that notion, she trotted off with Cisco in tow. Not that it mattered. We'd be back before she finished lunch anyway.

I said to Jolene, "You don't really want to see the place, do you? It's not illegal to target-shoot, and I already threw all the casings I could find into the weeds."

Willie put in, "If you want me to carry stuff down to the lake, I need to start loading it up." He looked as anxious to get to lunch as I was.

But Jolene ignored him and repeated, "Where did you find them?"

I sighed. "It's way over the hill in the old soccer field that we're using for agility." I glanced over my shoulder at Willie. "Come on, Willie, I'll show you which pieces of agility equipment we need."

But he looked annoyed and disgruntled as he stomped off in the other direction, muttering, "Gotta get the truck." I noticed he pulled out his cell phone as he stalked away, probably to complain to Margie.

I turned back to Jolene and, with a grand sweep of my arm, indicated the direction in which we should go. She was clearly accustomed to taking the lead, so I let her, falling into step beside her after a few strides.

The sun beat down upon my newly shorn head and I wished I had worn a cap. Of course, I had expected to be on my way to the nice cool dining hall by now, not tramping up a dirt road in the heat of the noonday sun. Nonetheless, I decided to try to make the best of it. "So how long have you and Nike been together?"

"Eight months."

Somehow I had thought it would have been longer than that. "Where did you work before this? Is this your first civilian job?"

"What difference does it make?"

I shrugged. "Just trying to be friendly, that's all." We walked a little farther, the hot trail crunching under our feet, and I said, "So how did you end up here?"

"God," she muttered under her breath, "do you *ever* shut up?"

I tried to count to ten, but only made it to five. "Look," I said tightly, "if you don't mind some advice…"

Rather predictably, she replied, "I do."

Also predictably, I ignored her. "This is a kid's camp. They ask questions. A lot of questions. That's what they do. You're here to answer them—politely and intelligently. That attitude of yours is going to get you nowhere fast."

"I'm here," she replied shortly, "because I was ordered to be. And I don't need a lecture on attitude from some smart-ass white bitch."

I stopped and stared at her. I couldn't believe she'd said that. And, judging by the quick look that flickered over her face, she couldn't either. The hard mask was back in an instant and she returned my gaze like a street fighter daring his opponent to make the first move. But this was not a fight in which I wanted to be involved. And though she didn't know it yet, neither did she.

I said in a voice that was almost normal, "In case you haven't noticed, we have all kinds of kids here—Asian, African American, Hispanic—so I think everyone would appreciate it if you would lose the racial slurs. And watch your language. You're not in the army now." I made a terse gesture toward the white ring gating that could be seen just beyond the rise. "Over there."

For the first time I saw something that might have been embarrassment cross her face. She looked as though she wanted to say something, but whatever it was, her lips tightened against it and she looked away. We resumed walking. Nike panted between us, the sun gleaming off her coat.

In a moment, she said, "Look, I know you're used to being the boss's little princess—"

I interrupted with a short bark of laughter. I'd been called a lot of things, including what she'd just called me two minutes earlier, but "princess" was a new one.

"But the last thing I'm interested in is your hokey small-town relations, where Billy-Bubba the mayor hires his brother Billy-Bob as police chief and both of them look the other way while Billy-Joe sells crack on the schoolyard because they're damn brothers. And yeah, you can tell your ex I said it. He'd've already fired me if he could anyhow."

I was of course intrigued by that, but felt compelled to defend my heritage first. "In the first place, I don't know a single person in this whole county named Billy-Bubba. And in the second place, if anybody even thought about selling crack on a schoolyard around here every man in the sheriff's department would be on him like a flock of ducks on a June bug and if you don't already know that you deserve to be fired and if Buck can't figure out a way to do it I'll be glad to help him!" My nostrils were flared and my breath was coming hard, and it was from more than the climb or the heat. "This *is* a small town, and yes, everybody knows each other, and yes, we do things a little differently than you're used to in the big city, but we get them done. Like it or not, you're part of that small town now—worse, you represent it!—so you'd better get with the program. And smile at the damn kids every now and then, will you?"

I pushed aside a length of ring gating and gestured angrily. "Here," I said. "Knock yourself out. I'm going to lunch."

She unclipped Nike's leash as I turned away, and I couldn't resist a lingering peek at Nike's technique. It spoiled my dramatic exit, I know, but, my goodness, that dog was magnificent at work. I couldn't take my eyes off her as she crisscrossed the scent path, moving like liquid across the small fenced area and, when Jolene removed a far gate for her, straight into the weeds toward the hay bale target, and beyond, probably scenting where I'd tossed the shells. She could really track scent objects that old? And that scattered? Despite myself, I was intrigued. I followed at a distance, and was glad that Jolene didn't even notice.

The terrain of the land was such that the high fescue grass and brambles gave way to scrub pine and tangled boulders after a couple hundred yards. Beyond that was a sharp rocky incline that led up to the bridle path and the forest beyond. You could easily reach the path if you were a mountain goat. If you weren't, you would come to a dead stop at the bottom of the cliff, where the rocky boulders had fallen when the road was cut above. That's precisely what Nike did. She stopped. She sat and she barked.

There was no way any of the spent shell casings I had thrown had made it this far. I increased my pace until I was jogging.

When I reached Jolene, she was shining a flashlight into a small crevice she had created by digging away some of the loose rock around the boulder pile. Nike chewed her rope toy and looked pleased with herself. Jolene said, without looking back at me, "I thought you were going to lunch."

I said, following the beam of her flashlight, "It looks like something is buried under there."

She didn't answer, just started pulling aside more of the loose rocks. I helped her, and in a matter of minutes we'd uncovered a flap of dusty green fabric. We moved a few more rocks, widening the hole to about two feet across, and Jolene pulled out what proved to be a green canvas bag, half filled with something that rattled as it was dragged across the stones and set on the ground. Nike moved close as Jolene unzipped the bag.

"Holy cow," I said, staring. "Are those..."

"M67s." Jolene sat back on her heels, her expression grim. "Fragmentation grenades."

I took a step back, still staring. There were two dozen of them or more, round, green bombs with a lever and a pull pin attached to the brass-capped bottleneck. They were somehow smaller than I had imagined, not that I'd spent a great deal of time imagining what a hand grenade would look like. The ugliness of them all piled together inside the canvas bag was profound. My voice sounded a little hoarse as I said, "But—they can't be real. What are they doing here?"

Jolene had turned back to the opening in the rocks, exploring the inside with her flashlight beam. I could tell now that the way the boulders had fallen created a natural cave of sorts that extended four or five feet back to the bank. Someone had disguised the opening by gathering up the smaller stones and wedging them between the boulders. As I looked around, feeling chilled in the bright sunlight, I noticed something else that had only registered with me peripherally before now. The grass had been flattened in long rows leading up to and away from the place we were standing. Those were tire tracks, and they had been made since the rain yesterday.

What kind of vehicle could traverse this terrain without getting stuck? A tractor. A jeep. An ATV. And only one of those could crisscross this camp at will without anyone giving it a second glance.

Willie had been standing right beside me when Nike alerted. No, not beside me, almost in back of me. What if it hadn't been the day-old shell casing that had triggered Nike, but something stronger, more recent...

Jolene crawled down from the opening in the boulders and stood up, clipping the flashlight back onto her utility belt and brushing off her hands on her pants. "There are half a dozen cases of ammunition in there, and some other things under tarps I can't see. I need to call this in. We'll have to evacuate the camp. Go back and let them know."

I nodded slowly, my mind whirring, my heart beating slow and hard. "I just don't understand why—"

"Raine!" I spun at the sound of Melanie's voice, and there she was, red-faced, sweating, and looking enormously pleased with herself as she crossed the field from the agility ring, Cisco pulling on the end of the leash. "Cisco tracked you all the way here!" she called happily. "He really did! He didn't want to go in the ex-pen," she added.

It was at this point I found my voice enough to cry, "Melanie, stop! Stay back!"

She slowed down about a hundred feet away, but didn't stop. "What's up?" she called back.

Out of the corner of my eye, I saw Jolene take out her cell phone, but it was at that moment Cisco spotted Nike and lunged toward us with excitement, jerking the leash out of Melanie's hand. I drew a breath to shout at him, but the words never made it out of my mouth. There was a deafening crack of an explosion. I cried out and staggered back, and when I looked down my tee shirt was spattered with blood.

# Chapter Twenty

I could see Cisco, a blur of gold and terror, barreling toward me. I could see Melanie right behind him. I could see Jolene on the ground, grasping her arm across her chest, and I realized the blood was hers. Nike stood stiffly at attention, her eyes on something beyond my shoulder. I turned my head and saw a soldier running toward us, rifle in hand and pointed at us.

All of this registered in less time than it takes to take a breath. Cisco was still running. Melanie was still stumbling toward us. Nike was poised and ready, her eyes on the soldier who was now less than ten feet from us. Jolene shouted hoarsely through gritted teeth, "Nike, Fa—"

I knew it was the command to attack even though she never finished the syllable. As she spoke, I saw the soldier swing his gun toward Nike and I screamed, "No!" I whirled toward Nike, stumbled and fell to one knee, putting my body between hers and the rifleman's as I grabbed her collar with one hand and flung my other arm around her neck. "*Nike, nein!*"

It was the only German word I knew and I had no real notion that this highly trained police dog would obey my command over her handler's. Very likely she would not have, but my voice drowned out Jolene's in that crucial moment and she screamed at me, "Are you crazy? Let her go! Nike—"

But then the soldier was upon her, drawing back his booted foot and slamming it into her head. Her body jerked violently with the impact and was still. I made a sound; I pressed my face into Nike's shoulders, tightening a fist in her fur. In a blur of motion, the soldier wrested Jolene's firearm from its holster, then tore a strip of duct tape from the roll on his own belt and pressed it over her mouth. He jerked her bloody hand behind her back and bound it to the other one with another strip of tape. Everything was etched in slow-motion detail, but it all happened so fast my brain couldn't register what my senses took in. There was blood on the ground, blood on Jolene's clothes, blood on me. The sound of hysterical barking bore down on me as Cisco's claws tore up clods of earth in his frantic race to reach me. Melanie was so close now I could hear her gasping breaths, and I wanted to scream *Melanie, no! Run the other way! Go back!* but if I did, would the soldier swing his rifle on her? Nike strained against my grip and Melanie and Cisco were close, closer, and it was too late to scream now, too late to stop them, I couldn't even draw in a breath. The soldier shoved Jolene's gun into his waistband and tore the radio off her belt, then kicked away the remnants of her cell phone that had been shot from her hand. I thought he would shoot her then, but instead he swung the rifle toward Cisco, who was bearing down on us in a fury of terrified barking.

I screamed, "Cisco, *down!*"

For three years we had practiced the emergency down with the same religious fervor with which we had practiced the emergency come. The thing about an emergency command is that you never know how effective your training has been until it has been tested in an emergency, and then there is no room for error. It will either save your dog's life, or it won't.

This time it did.

Cisco took one or two more galloping steps, just enough time for the command to reach him and register in his brain, and then he slid to the ground a half dozen yards in front of me, panting. Melanie stumbled toward me and I opened an arm for her, drawing her close and holding on tight to Nike's collar with the other hand, thinking, *Cisco, stay, stay, stay, please just stay...*and ducking my head involuntarily as the soldier jerked his rifle toward me. Melanie's quick hot breath hissed in my ear and her tee shirt was damp with sweat; I could feel the rabbit-fast pounding of her heart, or maybe it was my own. She gasped, big-eyed, "Is that real blood? Is that lady...is she dead?"

I understood then that Melanie, so comfortable in the world of television violence and video games, must have thought until this moment that this was all

part of the demonstration, a drama staged to enter-
tain the children and her only concern was that she
not be left out. Maybe it was the blood, or maybe it
was my wet face and shuddering breaths, but only
now was she beginning to suspect this might not be a
game. I whispered, "No. She—she's not dead." I did
not know that to be true. I hoped it was. But I didn't
know. "Be still, Mel. Just, just be real—be really still,
okay?"

The soldier was wearing a half-face respirator
mask with filters on either side and full goggles with
a polarized tint that hid his eyes. His head was covered by a billed cap of the same camouflage material
that comprised his shirt and pants. His chest was rising and falling rapidly and I could hear his breath,
but the rifle that was trained on us was steady and
unwavering.

"Is that a real soldier?" asked Melanie. Her voice
was quiet with awe. "Is there a war?"

I swallowed hard. My eyes were on Cisco. *Please,
please, please...* "I don't know," I managed. I found
her hand and squeezed it. Nike shifted her weight,
straining forward. My fingers were growing numb
around her collar. "I don't...know."

There was a sudden crackling sound that made
us all jump. Cisco's ears swiveled forward, and I
realized the sound was coming from a small radio
clipped to the soldier's collar. A tinny voice said,
"North sentry, report."

"Two adult females, one child, two canines."
The soldier's voice was muffled by the respirator,

but chillingly audible. "Situation secure. Request instructions re: disposition."

"Hold your position. Mission accelerated. Repeat: mission accelerated. ETA on reinforcements, sixty seconds."

It was all like something out of a really bad movie. Except that it wasn't.

"You." The soldier jerked his head at me. "Get leashes on those dogs. You try anything funny and I'll shoot them."

I said, "I won't do anything dumb, really." I got unsteadily to my feet, still gripping Nike's collar. "Don't shoot them. They're pets. They won't hurt anybody. They're good dogs."

"Raine?" Melanie's voice had a high, tight quality to it and she wouldn't let go of my hand as I tried to move away to retrieve Nike's leash. Her eyes were fixed upon the barrel of the gun that was still pointed at her.

I said unsteadily, "It's okay. Stay here. I'm just going to get Nike's leash." I shifted my eyes toward the leash, which Jolene had draped around her neck and which had become half-pinned by her body when she fell. I said deliberately to the soldier, "Okay?"

He nodded curtly and I pulled my hand away from Melanie's grip. Cisco watched me with anxious, impatient eyes. *Please, boy, please my good dog, please just a few more minutes.* The long down in an AKC obedience trial was three minutes. Cisco had never made it.

I stretched across the distance between us, holding on to Nike's collar, and knelt beside Jolene. I heard her muffled moan as I gently tugged the handle of the leather leash from beneath her hip. I could see, now that I was this close, that the blood was coming from her hand, and it was a mangled mess. But you couldn't die from a bullet wound to the hand. Could you? The side of her jaw was swollen and red from the imprint of the boot, and a trickle of blood ran from her ear. But she moved her head, and her eyes seemed to flutter behind closed lids. She was alive. And there was nothing I could do for her except to try my best to keep her that way.

I stepped quickly back to Melanie and snapped the leash onto Nike's collar, winding it tight around my hand. I took a breath, straightened my shoulders and called as matter of factly as I was able, "Cisco, come."

Cisco was not fooled. He knew perfectly well there was nothing matter of fact about the situation, the gun, the man with the mask, the blood and smell of fear that must have been radiating off of me and Melanie in waves. But my good dog stood up, tail wagging low and trailing his leash, and trotted over to me. I started breathing again when I took his leash in my hand.

The soldier said, "Take off your pack. Toss it over here."

I transferred both leashes to one hand, but my fingers were shaking so badly it took three tries to release the catch on my fanny pack. I tossed it underhanded toward him. It landed at his feet and he left it there.

"Turn out your pockets," he said.

I did. Cisco watched me, looking for treats. Nike never took her eyes off the soldier.

He said, "The kid too."

Melanie looked at me and I nodded. She pulled the white lining of her shorts' pockets outward. Then she unclipped the bait pouch from her belt loop and held it out to him in open hand. "You want this too?" Her voice was small, her eyes big behind the glasses. "It's just dog treats."

"Toss it over here."

She did. The little pouch landed a few feet short of my pack, and he let it lie there. An amateur would have bent to pick them both up. This guy had training.

I clenched my muscles in dread as I heard the ATV engine chugging up the rise, not knowing whether I should be relieved or horrified to see Willie at its helm. If I was wrong about him, he could be coming to our rescue. But if I was right...

But it turned out it didn't matter. The man behind the wheel was not Willie but another soldier, dressed in combat gear and wearing the same half-face respirator mask, goggles and bill cap as was the first man. He swung out of the vehicle and turned a rifle on us while the first soldier searched my pack. He removed my cell phone and radio and pocketed them, then opened Melanie's pouch. Finding nothing, he tossed both onto the floorboard of the ATV's wagon. He jerked his gun toward Jolene, who was still on the ground, though semiconscious now and moaning.

"What are our orders?"

"Take her with us," said the other man. "Command thinks she might be useful."

"What about the dogs?"

The way he said it, the way he turned his rifle so casually toward Cisco and Nike, made my blood run cold. Melanie leaned into me.

The other man said, "Secure them with the others. This is not our mission."

One of the soldiers pulled Jolene to her feet. Nike's head swiveled toward her handler and I held onto her leash so tightly my arm trembled. The soldier pushed Jolene into the wagon, but she couldn't sit with her hands bound behind her and she fell to her knees on the floorboard. I saw the whites of her eyes as they rolled back in pain. The soldier jerked her upright again. The other man pointed his gun at me. "Get in," he commanded.

Melanie climbed in before me. Cisco jumped into the cart immediately and sat at Melanie's feet, panting heavily, but Nike balked when I took her collar and tried to urge her in. The soldier jerked his rifle toward her impatiently. I said, "Hup!" only hoping it was the command she had been trained to, and it was. Nike climbed in beside Cisco and I followed quickly. I picked up my fanny pack and strapped it around my waist; I don't know why. I remember thinking it had my driver's license in it, like that mattered, and twenty dollars for the camp store. You do strange things when the whole world suddenly spins crazily out of control in front of your eyes.

One soldier started the engine and turned the vehicle back toward the lodge. The other stood on the running board, his rifle trained on us and unwavering. I held the dogs' leashes tightly in one hand and Melanie's hand in the other, just as tightly. No one spoke a word or dared to move the entire way back.

# CHAPTER TWENTY-ONE

If there was one thing Buck had learned about being a good leader it was the importance of knowing your strengths. His strengths were not research, or computer analysis, or studying smart screen projections until his eyes bled. The FBI was good at that. He left them to it and did what he did best: solving problems.

As far he could tell, the most urgent problem was finding out what, if anything, the insurgents planned to blow up on the Fourth of July. And the fastest way to do that was to talk to somebody on the inside. And the fastest way to do that was to find out who murdered Carl Brunner. So far the only lead in that case had been Reggie Connor.

But then, in the process of cleaning out his inbox that morning, which was something he tried to do every four or five days whether it needed it or not, he came across a complaint filed Thursday night by a resident of Camelback Road, a dirt switchback in the middle of nowhere that boasted precisely two taxpaying residents: Abe Kale and Henry Middleton. The taxpaying part was what Abe

Kale took pains to emphasize when he complained about all the cars barreling down the road toward his neighbor's house, blowing up dust into his hen-house and upsetting his laying hens. The officer who took the report reminded Abe that there was no law against a fellow having company to which Abe replied that there ought to be a law about how many cars should be allowed to park in one fellow's yard because there must've been twenty or thirty of them down at Henry Middleton's house. The officer did his duty by driving down to the end of the road where the Middleton property was and reported no cars in the yard and only one—license plate belonging to Henry Middleton—in the driveway.

That was the first thing that struck Buck. The complaint had been called in at eight thirty. The report had been filed at ten-oh-five. Generally if a man was having a party with twenty or thirty guests it lasted more than an hour. The second thing that caught his interest was that Henry Middleton was Reggie Connor's cousin.

The FBI had asked them to keep an eye out for unauthorized assemblies and, even though the order had made his skin crawl when he first heard it, reeking as it did of edicts issued by every dictator from Hitler to Hussein, he dutifully copied the report and e-mailed it to Manahan. He then decided to have a talk with Henry Middleton himself.

That was what he was on his way to do when the radio crackled and Wyn's voice reported, "This is Unit Six. We have a visual on a red oh-three Jeep

Wrangler NC license PAT0845. Vehicle is parked outside Banks' General Store on Indian Drum Mountain Road."

That was Reggie Connor's plate. Before he could respond, Lyle Reston's voice broke in, "Unit Two, ETA ten minutes."

He was closer than Buck was, so Buck said, "Silent approach, Unit Two. Keep the vehicle under surveillance. Unit One en route, ETA twenty."

"Roger," Wyn said. Then, "Say, Buck, doesn't Willie usually open on Saturdays this time of year?"

Buck replied, "Last I heard."

She said, "The Closed sign is in the window."

Buck frowned, but couldn't explain it anymore than she could. He punched on the flasher bar and accelerated to eighty.

I tried to count the soldiers I saw as we pulled up in front of the Rec Hall but I couldn't. Ten? Fifteen? All I could see were the assault rifles, the gas masks, the combat boots. Melanie whispered, "Maybe they're making a movie."

But I think even she finally understood that whatever was going on was desperately real when the two soldiers escorted us at gunpoint up the steps and into the Rec Hall. One of the soldiers held on to Jolene's arm to keep her upright.

The door opened upon a cacophony of barking dogs and crying children. The five adults and three teenage counselors were sitting on the floor against the wall while a soldier stood in front of them with his feet planted and his gun leveled at them. The children were against the opposite wall, although I noticed the soldier who guarded them stood in the arms-at-rest position, which, while it was no less terrifying, was at least not quite as much a direct threat. One little boy cried, "I'm not afraid of you! My daddy will beat you up!" and then he burst into tears. "Don't hurt Panda! Don't hurt my dog!"

Another child sobbed, "I want to go home. My mommy said I could go home…"

And everyone, adults and children, swiveled their heads toward us when the door opened and we stumbled in. A collective sob of horror seemed to go around the room when they saw the police officer bound, gagged and bleeding. Even the barking of the dogs became more hysterical.

Someone shoved me hard on the shoulder. "Get those dogs in cages."

The other soldier pushed Jolene into a sitting position against the wall. Her head lolled. I could tell she was about to pass out. A plump woman in a white uniform spoke up. She was the camp nurse, whose name I had never even known. It was Kathy, I learned later, and simply by speaking up at that moment she became one of the bravest women I had ever known.

Beneath the generalized fear and disbelief in her voice, there was a note of sharp alarm as she looked at Jolene. "She can't breathe! Can't you take the tape off?"

The soldier stared at me and I understood. Until Nike was secure, he was taking no chance that Jolene might order her attack dog into action. I said quickly, breathlessly, "Okay. Yes, I will. Right now."

Melanie clung to me. "I need to see Pepper. Can't I—"

"Melanie, stop!" I jerked away from her, my heart pounding my tone sharp. "Go sit with Counselor Haley. Now!"

I clucked my tongue to Nike and Cisco and led them away at a brisk clip, not wasting a moment to see if Melanie complied. The dogs' excited barking accelerated as I approached with the two strange canines, and by instinct I shouted in my booming kennel voice, "*Dogs! Quiet!*" In the face of authority, the dogs were reassured, as they usually are, and all but a couple of yippy terriers settled down.

I found an empty crate against the wall and led Nike into it, unclipping her leash and snapping it onto the side of the crate. The average person might think that at this point I would have thought of some heroic measure that would release Nike into action and save us all. The average person might think that the last thing I would have been so meekly willing to do was to lock up our only hope in a steel cage. The average person has never been held hostage at gunpoint by a roomful of soldiers in gas masks with automatic weapons.

There were no more empty crates, so I had to put Cisco in the ex-pen with Pepper. Pepper wanted to escape and Cisco did not want to go in, so I had to drag him by the collar while holding a bucking Pepper with the other hand. I finally got them both inside and shot the bolts on the exercise pen. I scanned the room for Mischief, and found her, looking alert and interested but completely unruffled in a crate on the other side of the room. Lee knew about her propensity for unlocking doors and had secured her crate with two heavy-duty snap clips. I breathed a sigh of relief that all three of my dogs were safe—Magic being the safest, back in my cabin—and turned to walk away.

The next thing I knew all the dogs were barking again and I heard the scrabble of claws on the cement floor behind me. I turned to see Cisco racing toward me. The dog trainer in me sprang into action and I held up my hand, palm out, in the automatic "distance come" signal. Cisco skidded to a sit in front of me.

I had absentmindedly looped Cisco's leash around my neck when I left him, just as Jolene had done when she'd released Nike to find her target. Now I bent to quickly clip the leash to his collar and when I looked up a rifle barrel was pointed at my cheek.

It was at that point that I did the only heroic thing I'd done throughout the episode and it was, of course, in defense of my dog. "He's a golden retriever, for God's sake!" I cried. Cisco panted his most endearing pant at my feet. "He's harmless!"

Golden retrievers are the second—or maybe it's the third?—most popular breed in the AKC. The soldiers in their Darth Vader masks who surrounded us now might be twisted, messed-up, trained killers today, but the chances are that at one point in their lives some of them had owned, and been loved by, a golden retriever. Or had at least known one.

When I found myself still alive after my outburst, I pressed my advantage. "He doesn't like to be crated," I pleaded. "He won't stay. But I can keep him out of your way. He's a good dog. Look." I then gave Cisco his oldest, and most reliable, advanced command. Still, I held my breath until he completed it. "Cisco, go place."

I pointed toward the wall where Melanie was being comforted against the shoulder of Counselor Haley. Cisco looked uncertain for a moment, but he must have been moved by the deity of dogs to whom my prayers had been forwarded, because he got up, trotted over to the wall, found an empty place close to Melanie, and lay down.

"Please," I repeated. My breath came light and fast. "He's a good dog."

After a moment, he lowered the gun. "Over there," he said, and gestured toward the wall where the adults were seated.

I sank to my knees in front of Jolene and, without thinking, ripped off the duct tape from her mouth. She sagged back against the wall, gasping for breath. Kathy, the nurse, got up and came over to us. She touched Jolene's forehead and then swung her head around to the soldier nearest. "I need a first aid kit," she said. "There's one in the restroom."

The soldier was impassive.

"She's unarmed," I said. "Her dog is confined. Let us help her."

He said nothing. But he made no move to stop her as Kathy moved quickly to the restroom.

Jolene, breathing hard, focused angry eyes on me. "Are you—crazy?" she demanded at last in a hoarse rasp. "Why did you stop her?"

It took my poor battered brain a moment to wind back the reel of the past few incredible moments to find the incident to which she referred. "He would have shot her!"

"And then I would have shot him," she said through gritted teeth. "I could have stopped this. Nike...could have stopped this. We're here... because of you."

My hands and feet started to tingle with cold, the shock was that severe. I stared at her. *My fault, my fault...*I sat back on my heels. "What kind of person sends her dog to die?" I whispered.

"That's her job!" Jolene spat at me, her chest heaving. "These dogs are not pets...they're weapons! Damn it..." Her head sank back against the wall and her eyes closed. "I could have stopped this."

Indian Drum Mountain Road was one of those long country roads that led nowhere, dotted by pretty valley farms and horses behind unpainted fences, white farmhouses and rickety barns. There were signs for campgrounds, boiled peanuts and fresh produce, and in the summertime Banks General Store did a brisk business supplying tourists with bundles of campfire wood and jugs of water, not to mention all the kitschy things nobody left the mountains without buying: jars of homemade preserves with checkered cloths tied over the caps, waterfall guide maps, stick candy from a big jar and tee shirts with pictures of bears on them. But when Buck pulled up, the Jeep Cherokee was the only car in the gravel lot; the two Hanover County Sheriff's Department vehicles were idling nose-to-nose on the berm across the road.

When he got out of the car, Les and Wyn pulled their unit behind the Jeep, blocking its exit, and Lyle, who was riding alone today, pulled in on the other side. The three deputies got out. Buck peered inside the windows; Lyle checked the passenger door. "Unlocked," he reported.

Buck grunted an acknowledgement, but made no attempt to open the car door. Nothing that he saw inside gave him cause to.

He walked around the jeep to the front of the store. "Les, you and Wyn check around back. Lyle, see if there's a side entrance."

As his deputies dispersed, Buck shook the locked door handle. "Willie!" he called out. "You okay? You're missing business out here!"

He peered in the front windows and saw movement in the shadows. He stepped away from the door as Lyle opened it. "The delivery entrance was unlocked," he explained.

Buck stepped inside and glanced around for a light switch. He found it and a bank of overhead fluorescents flickered on, illuminating four short aisles stocked with merchandise, a cash register, and not much else. "Willie!" he called out again. "Sheriff Lawson! Are you here?"

They split up and started to walk the aisles, but hadn't made it much past the end caps when Les came in from the back, his expression grim. "You won't find him here, Sheriff," he said. "He's sitting in his truck out back with a bullet hole in his head. And Buck," he added before Buck could react, "you need to see what's under the tarp in the back of his pickup."

# CHAPTER TWENTY-TWO

Cisco had managed to creep forward until his head was in Melanie's lap. I left Kathy to do what she could for Jolene's injuries and went to sit beside them. Melanie's head was bent forward as she stroked Cisco's head, and her tangled hair obscured her face, but I saw a tear form a dark blotch on Cisco's fur. I said, "I'm sorry I snapped at you, Melanie." My throat hurt with the effort to speak. Everything inside me hurt. She was just a kid, frightened and alone, and I was supposed to protect her. Instead I had yelled at her. "I was scared."

After a moment, she nodded. "Me too," she whispered. And then, brokenly, "I want my mom!"

"I know," I said. I tried to smile. "But hey, you're going to see her in a couple of weeks, right? And you're going to love Brazil." I frantically tried to remember something about Brazil and came up with a scrap of a documentary I had seen on television. "Parrots fly wild in the streets there, and they have these festivals where guys put on ten-foot-tall stilts and wear long ruffled dresses and big hats and walk in parades."

Melanie sniffed. "I think that's Argentina."

She would know.

She pushed up her glasses, wiped her eyes with her fingers and looked up at me. She sniffed. "I'm sorry I cried." Her eyes were still swimming and her voice was broken. "I don't want my daddy to go to war! What will happen to Pepper and me?"

I scooted close and put an arm around her shoulders, pulling her into me. She was trembling with the effort not to sob out loud. I said, with all the firmness I could muster, "Your dad is not going to war. I promise you that. I don't think..." I looked around the room uneasily. There were four men in combat gear with rifles, one guarding the children, one guarding the adults, another standing over Jolene and Kathy and one guarding the door. The soldier guarding us marched up and down our little row, and every time he did the dogs would launch themselves into a new frenzy of barking, giving cover to our voices. Cisco's ears remained permanently pricked with the commotion, but he was not about to leave Melanie's side. "I don't think these are real soldiers."

Haley, the counselor who had been trying to comfort Melanie, overheard this. "But those are real guns, aren't they?" Streaks of mascara across her white cheeks betrayed her own tears, and she still looked terrified.

I said, "Yes." My arm tightened around Melanie's shoulders.

Haley watched as the soldier guarding us walked down the row. When his back was to us, she said shakily, "Why are they wearing gas masks? Are they—do you think they're going to gas us?"

"No," I said quickly, aware of Melanie's frightened gaze on me. In fact, I thought that was exactly what they planned to do; it was cleaner and easier than shooting and why else would they be wearing respirators? But as I spoke I found I was convincing myself. "They have no reason to do that. I think—I think the masks and goggles are for disguise, so we can't describe them later. And if we can't describe them, we're no threat to them. They have no reason to kill us."

The other two teenagers were listening, and all of them, including Melanie, looked anxious to believe that. So was I.

Haley whispered, "They shot the police woman."

I nodded, and shifted my glance toward Jolene. "She's okay." She did not look okay. One eye was swollen almost completely shut and her lip was split and as the nurse tried to clean and bandage her hand, her face had gone an ashy color I had never seen on a human before. I said, "And she's supposed to report back to duty in a couple of hours. When the sheriff's department doesn't hear from her, they'll know something is wrong and they'll send somebody out. We'll be okay."

I hoped I was the only one who heard the hollowness of that. A single team of deputies against a dozen men with automatic rifles? They'd be walking into a massacre.

Margie, sitting next to Haley, said anxiously, "We can't keep these kids calm for two hours. They're practically hysterical now."

Her husband Steve said lowly, "There are as many of us as there are of them. If we…"

"No," I said sharply, and Margie hissed at the same time, "Shut up, Steve! They have guns!"

Bill ventured uncertainly, "Twenty-five dogs. If we let them all out…"

I shook my head adamantly, remembering how effortlessly the soldier had turned his gun on Cisco and Nike. "No. No, we don't want to do anything to start gunfire, because once we do there's no going back. Just…we just have to stay calm. We don't know what they want yet."

"She's right," Lee said. "This is not a random thing. They waited until lunch time, when all the dogs were crated and all the kids and most of the adults were in one place. They knew it would be easier to move us all in here that way. They didn't even search the kids for phones. They must've known they're all locked up in the office during the day. This was well thought out, carefully planned. They've got to have a reason for it. We just have to wait and find out what it is."

The soldier had turned and was walking back toward us. I spotted a half-empty bottle of water on the windowsill above my head, and I pointed to it, then inclined my head toward Jolene. I raised my voice to be heard above the din. "Can I take it to her?"

He paused, then stepped back. I tried my best to get a look at his face, even the smallest of glimpse of something that might let me guess his age. Nothing.

I told Cisco to stay, and added to Melanie, "Hold on to him, okay?" just as I had done dozens of times before, just as though it was just another normal day, just as though walking those six or seven steps from here to Jolene didn't mean taking my life in my hands.

Kathy had just finished wrapping Jolene's hand in gauze, and when I knelt beside her she handed me a roll of adhesive tape. "Tear off some strips, will you? About three inches long. They took the scissors."

I started tearing the tape into strips and handing them to Kathy. Jolene avoided my eyes.

"It's not as bad as it looks," the nurse said. She tried to smile at Jolene. "A couple of broken fingers, but the bullet just tore the fleshy part of the thumb. We need to get you sewn up, but you'll be fine."

"The bastard was a marksman," Jolene muttered. "He shot the phone right out of my hand."

Of course that should have been my cue to make some remark about how she could blame me for saving Nike's life when she clearly could not have fired her weapon with a broken hand—or even held it— but I was too fixated on the word "marksman" to say anything for a moment. I tore off another strip of tape. I could feel the soldier's eyes on the back of my neck. I said as quietly as I could to her, "When are you due to report in?"

Jolene's lips compressed and she said nothing. She didn't have to. I could see it in her eyes.

I let the truth sink in, one horrible moment at a time. "You're not," I said at last, dully. I stared at her. "You have the weekend off. You lied."

No one was expecting her back. Buck wouldn't raise the alarm when she didn't report in. No one would know anything was wrong.

No one was coming for us.

Kathy must have grasped the significance of this as well as I did, because I saw a flash of alarm in her eyes which she quickly tried to hide. She turned back to the first aid kit and took out two small paper packets, tore them open and shook out the pills into Jolene's good hand. "All I have is ibuprofen," she said.

I took the cap off the water and handed it to Jolene as she popped the pills into her mouth. She drank. "Thanks." She made a small gesture with the bandaged hand and winced with the pain of it. "I'm okay now."

I said quietly, "Better keep that information to yourself. I think you and Nike are the only ones they're worried about here, and thinking they've put you out of commission might be the all that's keeping you alive."

Kathy's face was rigid with distress. "What do you think they want?"

Jolene looked from one to the other of us, a darting gaze that was disconcerting because of her one swollen eye. "There was a briefing this morning," she said. "The FBI uncovered a radical militia cell operating around here somewhere. One of their agents…" she swallowed hard, "a man named Carl Brunner, was killed trying to infiltrate them, and his body was placed in a stolen car and burned."

I caught my breath. "Jessie Connor's car."

She nodded. "That's one of the reasons Nike and I were assigned here. The FBI thought the terrorists were planning something for Monday, maybe something to do with Jeb Wilson's appearance, but that must've been a smokescreen. This was the real operation. The FBI never would have been expecting anything out here."

"My God," whispered Kathy.

"This must have been their training camp," I murmured. "And any of these buildings would have been a good place to store munitions." I glanced at Jolene. "I think Willie, the caretaker, might have been moving them this morning. He knew Nike was coming, but we all expected you later. And he didn't know we had moved the demo site down to the lake. He just didn't finish before Nike found the stash."

Kathy said uncertainly, "But…all these children! Why would anyone take all these children hostage?"

Jolene said simply, "Can you think of a better way to negotiate for something big?"

I felt the sharp jab of steel in my shoulder and I stiffened. What does it say about me that I know too well what the barrel of a gun pressed into my skin feels like? The soldier said harshly, "You! Make those dogs shut up!"

I got slowly to my feet. Kathy stopped fussing with the first aid kit and watched me. Jolene watched me too. I turned to face him. "They're dogs," I said. I couldn't believe how steady my voice was. "They're going to bark. If the kids weren't so upset, the dogs would quiet down."

"Do something!" he insisted. "You did it before."

I went over to the crating area, still clutching the roll of adhesive tape in my hand. The soldier followed a few steps behind. I unzipped my pack, dropped the roll of tape inside and took out my clicker and treats. I stopped in front of the first row of cages, bellowed again, "*Dogs! Quiet!*" And in the first breath of silence I clicked, dug into my bag of treats and tossed one into the first cage. The sheltie inside gobbled up the treat and sat, waiting for more. I moved quickly to the next cage, and the next, clicking and treating as dogs sat in anticipation down the line. When I got to Mischief, I gave her an extra treat and a kiss on the nose, whispering thickly, "Some vacation, huh, girl?" Pretty soon the only sound that could be heard was the sound of my clicker and the happy snuffling of treats. When I came to Nike's cage, I could practically hear the soldier's finger tighten on the trigger. I dropped a treat into her cage and moved on. She ignored it.

I had used that technique before to calm the kennel dogs, and it usually worked. Contentment among dogs is contagious, and as long as there is the expectation of something good coming their way, most dogs will wait for it. When the dogs were mostly calm, I turned to the soldier and said, "It won't last long. Why don't you let the kids sit beside their dogs? They all have clickers and treats. They can keep them quiet a lot longer than I can."

He jerked his head back toward the opposite wall where the adults were huddled. I swallowed hard but did not return to my place. Instead I took a step toward him. "Come on," I said, pleading, "they're kids and they're scared to death. Can't you…"

I heard Melanie cry shrilly, "Cisco!" and I whirled to see my dog trotting toward me, trailing his leash, wagging his tail and smiling his sweet smile, wondering why all those other dogs had gotten treats and he hadn't.

Before I could draw a breath for a command, the soldier swung around and leveled his rifle on my dog. I screamed something inarticulate and lunged at him while at the same moment Melanie surged forward, grabbing for Cisco's leash and stumbling hard. She fell, and someone grabbed my shoulder and spun me backward so hard I almost landed on my rear. He faced off against the other soldier and I heard him rasp through the mask, "Soldier! This is not our mission!"

I stumbled across the slippery cement floor to Cisco and Melanie, and only when I had one arm around my dog's neck and the other arm around Melanie did I cry angrily, "Is this what you do, then? You shoot children and innocent dogs? Is this what you trained for? Is this what you're so damn proud of?"

One of the soldiers—I couldn't tell them apart now—turned to me. His words were distinct even through the muffling mask. "Lady, you have no idea who we are. We're your saviors. We're the ones that're going to protect you when your government goes up in flames! We're the ones you'll be calling out to! One day you'll be thanking us."

I wanted to scream a profanity at him, but the children were watching me. Everyone was watching me. The dogs were barking again. I took Cisco's leash and Melanie's hand and hurried back to the wall with the other adults. I told Cisco to sit and reached into the treat bag with trembling fingers, feeding him treats one after the other until my heart stopped pounding.

Melanie sat close to me, her eyes big and terrified. "Raine," she whispered, "I think I did something bad."

I reached for her hand and gave it a quick reassuring squeeze. "It's okay, it's not your fault. Cisco gets away from me all the time…"

"No, it's not that." She shot a quick frightened glance toward the soldiers, who were too far away to hear us now beneath the renewed cacophony of barking dogs. "I didn't want to, but when I thought he was going to shoot Cisco, and I fell down, I didn't know what else to do." She looked up at me, the fright in her eyes magnified behind the glasses. She whispered, "I pushed my panic button."

There were ten or twelve vehicles now crowding the parking lot and lining the road in front of Banks General Store; Buck had stopped counting when the state ME's van arrived to process the body. There were crime scene photographers, evidence analysts, munitions experts. And far too many federal agents for him to even make an attempt to remember their names.

One such agent took a long look beneath the tarp that covered Willie's truck bed and remarked, "There's enough C4 and blasting caps here to blow up a small city." Then he glanced at Buck and added, "Sorry, Sheriff."

Buck said, "Yeah. Looks like that's what somebody had in mind, huh?"

"Could be," agreed the agent. "Could be they were planning on trading for something bigger."

Buck did not ask what the "something bigger" might be. He had a lot of guesses, and none of them were good.

The agent said, "We've got a truck on the way to transport this stuff to the command center. Can you spare us a couple of deputies to load it?"

"Yeah, sure." He glanced around for Manahan and didn't see him, but Wyn caught his eye. He excused himself to the nameless agent and made his way through the throng of lawmen and women— some looking busy, some looking lost—to Wyn.

She turned her shoulder to the crowd, indicating he should follow, and lowered her voice to keep the conversation private. Maybe it was paranoid, but it was something local officers had learned to do when federal authorities took over a case. She said, "So we may have some info on what Reggie's jeep is doing here. I made a few calls, and it looks like he'd been working part time at the store the last few days, keeping it open while Willie was helping out at the camp."

Buck frowned. "Was he still taking care of that place? I'd've thought he was too old ten years ago."

She shrugged. "Apparently the people who rented the place for the weekend thought he was still capable of mowing the grass and running errands. Anyway, neighbors say Reggie opened up the store at seven a.m. yesterday and closed it at seven p.m. last night. We've got a report that the parking lot was empty at nine p.m. so I'm guessing he came back here this morning to open up and never did. Or maybe he did and closed again. I haven't been able to track down anything after nine last night."

"Good work," Buck said. "Stay on it, will you? Let me know what you find out about Reggie's whereabouts after seven this morning."

She nodded and started to turn away.

"Hey," he said.

She looked back at him. His expression was surprised and pleased, and he was looking at her hand. Specifically, he was looking at the ring on the third finger of her left hand.

"What's this?" he said.

She pretended nonchalance, fluttering her fingers casually. "Just giving it a test run," she said. "You know. Seeing how it affects my speed and accuracy, that sort of thing."

"And?"

"So far, so good."

He could see her fighting with a grin, a battle she quickly won when her eyes focused on something over his shoulder. She said, "I'm on it, Sheriff." She walked away. He turned to meet Agent Manahan.

"We'll need everything your office has on this Henry Middleton," Manahan said. "We've got agents staked out at his house but so far he's a no-show. We tracked down some links to some moderate subversive groups, nothing to raise a flag until now, but he may be our best lead."

Buck said, "Hell, as far as I knew the most subversive group he was ever a member of was the Saturday Night Bible Study."

"Yeah, well, that's the way it goes. We're running down Reggie Connor. Nothing yet."

Buck nodded. "Neighbors say he was last seen here at seven last night, closing up the store. If you want my opinion, it might not be a bad idea to do a search of the area, given what happened to Willie and all."

Manahan nodded. "You'll want to call in your K-9 team. I've got search dogs on the way but it'll take them two, three hours to get here. Do you have anybody closer?"

Buck said, "Yeah. I'll give them a call." It wouldn't be the first time he ruined Raine's weekend.

For a moment Manahan just stood there, looking out over the terrain. The mountain vistas, the tall wildflower fields, the undulating valleys in the distance. "God's country," he said. "Doesn't seem right, does it?"

Buck knew the agent was referring to the bigger plot of terrorism, a pickup truck full of explosives, the ticking time-bomb of a subversive plan none of them could decipher. Buck was thinking about a man he used to know with a bullet through his head. He said, "It never does." And he went back to work.

I felt all the breath rush out of my lungs and I stared at Melanie. I almost blurted my astonishment out loud, then swiveled a quick glance over my shoulder toward the soldiers behind us. I whispered to Melanie, "You have a panic button?"

She nodded, her eyes as big and frightened as they had been the moment she'd first realized the guns were real. "It's on a necklace under my shirt. Dad makes me wear it all the time. He said it was for in case I was ever in big trouble. He said if I pushed it he'd come, no matter where he was, he'd come and save me." She darted her eyes around the room from soldier to soldier. "I didn't want the soldiers to shoot him. So I didn't push it. Until now. They won't shoot my dad, will they?"

My breath was coming quick and light. I said, "It doesn't work that way, Mel. The security people call the police, and then they call your dad. He's not in any danger. They'll call the police." They'd call the police, and the police would come...wouldn't they?

I looked across the room at the children. It had not occurred to me before, but a lot of them had wealthy parents. Maybe not as wealthy as Miles, but their parents had traveled across the Southeast and paid several thousand dollars to allow them to attend a weekend camp with their purebred dogs. How many of them might also have panic buttons?

I looked at Margie, who was looking back at me with a kind of stunned understanding in her eyes. "Angela Bowers has a medical alert button," she said softly, quickly, "because of her allergies." She glanced at the soldiers, but they couldn't hear us over the barking of the dogs. "Josh Trenton, Ivy Winters, Bonnie Clayton. That's one of the questions we ask on the registration form."

One call from a security company would send a squad car to investigate. But multiple calls from different sources would signal a mass emergency and generate an appropriate response. Without access to telephones, it was as close as we could hope to come to letting Buck know what was happening here. I glanced over at Jolene, hoping she had been able to follow the conversation. She gave a small, almost imperceptible nod of acknowledgement.

"Make sure they're silent," she advised quietly. Her swollen lips barely moved. Since I had to strain to hear what she was saying, I knew the soldier closest to us could not.

I took a breath, trying to calm myself, and looked again at the row of children against the wall. How long before one of them, like Melanie, remembered the panic button and pushed it, silent or not? What would happen if they triggered a personal alarm, or if they got caught? I took another breath. I smiled, a little unsteadily, at Melanie.

"Hey," I said, "remember when we found that meth lab on the Christmas tree farm last year? And last month when Cisco got dognapped?" I kept my voice very low, and spoke close to her ear. To the soldiers I hoped it looked as though I was still just comforting her.

She nodded slowly.

"I couldn't have gotten out of any of those messes without you," I said. "You're the coolest kid I ever met. And the bravest." I leaned back and held her gaze. "I need you to go talk to the kids with panic buttons. Don't let the soldiers find out what you're doing. Tell them to make sure they're on silent alarm, and to push their buttons without letting anybody see them do it, just like you did. Can you do that?"

She nodded, slowly, and started to stand up. "I can do it," she said.

I caught her hand, wanting to pull her back beside me again. "Make sure their buttons are on silent alarm," I repeated in a whisper. "And—don't get caught, okay?"

She nodded and stood up.

"Melanie."

She looked back at me.

"I love you."

She smiled. "I love you too," she said.

So easy for her. But it cost me my heart.

I clenched a fist in Cisco's fur as I watched her walk up to one of the soldiers and say, "I want to go sit with my friends."

He didn't try to stop her. I didn't think he would.

She walked over and sat down beside Angela Bowers, who was crying. She patted her hand, as though she were comforting her, and then said something to her. After a moment, Angela stopped crying. She looked at the soldier, then back at Melanie. She nodded, very slightly. I released a breath and couldn't watch anymore.

I was surprised to look down and see a dark hand next to mine on Cisco's back. Jolene had slipped into Melanie's place, sliding closer to me on the pretense of petting my dog. When I looked up at her, she said, "What I said before—it was out of line."

I tried to search back over the many uncalled-for things she'd said since we met. I said, "You're right. It was. I can't help being white."

She actually chuckled—or tried to. The effort clearly caused her pain and she winced. Nonetheless, she replied, "And I can't help being a bitch."

She looked at me, and I managed a smile.

"That's not what I meant," she said. She looked down at Cisco, and her voice was strained as she spoke. "What I said about this being your fault... I couldn't have gotten to my sidearm in time. Couldn't have fired it with this hand. He would have shot the dog, and then me, and probably you too."

I said, "I know." And then I had to add, very quietly, "I've spent my whole life, practically, teaching people that it's their job to take care of their dogs, to protect them. I know what you said is true, that Nike is a different kind of working dog than I'm used to. But I'll never understand how anyone could send her own dog to her death."

She was silent for a moment, petting Cisco with her one good hand. Then she said in a voice that was rough with emotion, "Nike isn't my dog." She didn't look at me. "My dog's name was Hawk, and he was killed fifty feet in front of me when he triggered an IED in Afghanistan. He saved my life, and the lives of everyone on that patrol. That was what he was trained for. We'd been together three years. He was my dog."

I felt my gut twist with remembered pain. My first SAR dog Cassidy had died a hero in my arms after completing her final mission. I still wasn't over it. I didn't think I ever would be.

Jolene went on quietly, "After that...I guess I had some kind of breakdown or something. They called it PTSD, and I spent the last six months of my tour in a VA hospital. When I got out, I heard about this program with Homeland Security. They pay for your training, your dog, your first year's salary, and they place you in a job. They give preference to vets. What else was I going to do? I asked to be assigned to one of the rural communities. God knows I wasn't ready for NYC, or even an international airport. Your ex was nice enough, but it was harder to get back into the swing of things than I thought. I was always afraid of screwing up, so I kept trying harder to prove myself...anyway, the sheriff got pissed when he found out I was reporting to somebody other than him and I saw my career going down the drain and I guess I took it out on you when I got here. But it was out of line."

I was confused. "What do you mean, reporting to someone else?" I whispered.

She shifted her gaze briefly to the soldier guarding us. "Carl Brunner was an undercover agent. I was supposed to be his contact."

I drew in a breath and let it out slowly. "Cripes."

We were silent for a time, as I tried to let the scope and the breadth of what was happening sink in. This wasn't a random event. It was an operation. And even Homeland Security had not been able to stop it.

She said, very quietly, "This is just the beginning, you know. Even if the panic buttons work, once they get here...they won't know what they're up against. They won't have any way of finding us, or getting to us if they could. Flash grenades, tear gas...they can't use them because of the kids. It'll be a stand-off."

That was the last thing I wanted to hear. I looked around quickly to make sure no one else had heard. Nerves were frazzled enough as it was.

"But...all these dogs, the children...there's no food in here and only a few gallons of water for the dogs. How long can they keep us here? How long can it last?"

She replied bleakly, "Did you ever hear of Waco?"

# CHAPTER TWENTY-THREE

Buck had left two messages for Raine, but didn't expect to hear back from her until she finished whatever class she was teaching and remembered to turn her phone back on. That might be within the hour, it might not be until tonight. She wasn't on his payroll and had no obligation to keep her phone on during a holiday weekend. But he was furious when he couldn't raise Jolene, either by radio or cell phone. She knew the situation. He had told her to remain on high alert. She might not be on duty but she was on call. Had she just walked off the job? If she hadn't, he vowed bitterly to himself, she had just worked her last day under his command. You don't turn off your phone in the middle of a crisis, not ever, not for any reason. Had she even gone to the damn camp? He was about to call into the office to send a squad car after her when his radio crackled on his private channel.

"Unit One, this is Dispatch."

He unclipped his radio and spoke into it. "Go ahead, Dispatch."

"Sheriff, have you been following the situation with the security alarm?"

The radio was on in his car but he had not been monitoring it. "Kind of busy out here, Sue Anne."

"Yes, sir. We had a personal-alarm-activated report at 2:45. I dispatched a unit to the GPS coordinates the security company gave me, but then I realized we already have three units in that vicinity. Between 3:00 p.m. and 3:10, I got four more calls from different security companies with the same GPS. Buck, it's right up the road from your location. Camp Bluebird. I called the camp office, and no one answered. Then I called the camp director's private cell, but it went straight to voice mail. That's a total of five panic buttons in less than half an hour and no way to confirm. I thought you'd want to know."

Raine. Jolene. Willie Banks with a bullet through his head. A camp full of children pushing their panic buttons. A truck bed filled with explosives and Camp Bluebird less than a mile away. *Christ,* he thought. His throat went dry. *Christ.*

He said, "Stand by, Dispatch."

He clicked off the radio and found Manahan on the phone only a few feet away. He walked over to him, his expression grim. He did not wait for the other man to get off the phone. "Agent Manahan," he said, "if you've got a SWAT team standing by, you'd better call them in. I think that big event you've been waiting for is here."

It was hot inside the building. The ceiling fans stirred the air and provided some relief, but with all the doors closed and so many bodies, canine and human, crowded inside during the muggiest part of the day, the temperature felt higher than it was. Most of the dogs had tired of barking, and lay panting in their cages. Some of the children were flushed and lethargic looking; others were just miserable and sweaty and restless. Margie had passed around a gallon jug of water for the children; there wasn't much left for the dogs. Thunder rolled in the distance, signaling the approach of the daily rain that would begin the afternoon cooling. A few dogs began to whine and paw restlessly at their crates.

Thunder, but nothing else from outside. No wail of sirens, no megaphoned voices calling for surrender. It had been over an hour since Melanie had first gone over to talk to the children. Had our plan even worked? Maybe it had. Maybe the camp was surrounded by sharpshooters and sheriff's deputies and SWAT teams right now, but Jolene was right, they couldn't get to us; there was nothing they could do. Or maybe the plan hadn't worked. Maybe no one even knew we were here.

Cisco panted beside me, his fur plastered to my sweaty leg. If we were miserable, the soldiers had to be even more so behind their face masks and goggles, carrying those heavy weapons. How long could they keep this up? They might look like soldiers and act like soldiers and, if Jolene was right, they may have trained as soldiers, but they were not soldiers. They didn't have the stamina or the discipline or the combat skills to see a difficult job through to the end. How long before exhaustion and tension and a roomful of cranky kids and barking dogs pushed somebody over the edge and the unthinkable happened?

For a while, the soldiers had allowed Haley and Bill to take the kids, one by one and with an armed escort, to the bathroom. Some of the kids thought that was cool and had asked to go more than once, but when their requests were ignored, the novelty soon wore off. No one had asked to take the dogs out for a toilet break. I think we all knew that wasn't going to happen.

Now that the dogs had quieted down, we were not able to talk among ourselves without being overheard. So, except for an occasional murmured word of reassurance, no one had said anything in a while. Jolene, next to me, rested her head against the wall with closed eyes. Her face was beaded with sweat, but so was mine. I hoped she was only pretending to be asleep, and not actually unconscious. She might be disarmed and disabled, but she was the closest thing to an authority figure we had.

The sun passed behind a cloud, darkening the room, and another roll of thunder boomed. Some of the dogs yipped and started to frantically paw at their cages. Steve started to get to his feet. "I can keep them quiet," he said to the soldier who immediately swung his gun on him. "I can calm them down."

The soldier rasped, "Sit down."

And Steve did.

A chorus of whines and barks began to assemble from the crating area. One upset dog was all it took to incite an entire kennel. I was sure the soldier regretted his decision to quash Steve.

Beneath the cover of barking, Jolene murmured, without opening her eyes, "Funny how they let your dog run loose."

I said, in quick defense of my dog, "Everyone knows golden retrievers are harmless. And Cisco is special. He has a way of making people like him."

Jolene said, still without opening her eyes, "Nothing in common with his handler, then."

I said, "Gee, and I thought we were friends."

But my mind was working, as she had no doubt intended it to do. I thought about Cisco tracking a homeless man through the forest, destroying his provisions, and then being forgiven. I looked across the room at Melanie, who sat with her knees drawn up to her chest, frightened and forlorn. I thought about the three month stand-off in Waco, Texas. I whispered to Jolene, "What would they need to know?"

She replied, her eyes still closed, "Location, number of guns, points of access." I saw her throat convulse as she swallowed. "That we're alive. Mainly... that we're alive."

I sat there for a while longer, trying to talk myself out of what I knew I had to do. The room grew darker as the clouds built up, and the air grew thicker. When the rain came, it would be too late.

Finally, I swallowed hard and took Cisco's leash in my hand. I pushed myself to my feet and I looked the soldier in the eye and I said, "I need to go to the bathroom."

He didn't move for a long time and I thought he would deny me. After all, a bunch of whiny children was one thing, but why should they care whether or not the adults were comfortable? Then he gestured with his gun toward the restroom. He said, "Leave the dog."

"He won't stay with anyone but me," I said. "Besides, he has to go out, too." I nodded toward the crated dogs. "They all will, pretty soon."

Of course, I had no way of guessing his expression beneath the mask, but I could imagine it was annoyed. "Go," he said.

The restroom had three stalls and I took the one farthest from the entrance, where the soldier was stationed with his gun. It was a ridiculous redundancy, since the only form of egress was the high slated windows. Even if someone could scale the twenty-foot wall, the windows were too narrow for even a child to fit through. Or a dog.

I rummaged through my fanny pack and found the items I remembered to be there: the Sharpie I had used to label the kids' scent containers in Canine

Nosework class that morning—had it only been that morning?—and the roll of white adhesive tape I had absently dropped into my pack when I took out the clicker and treats earlier. The treats were gone, but the last thing I needed was still there. Working quickly, I wrote on the tape: 911 REC HALL KIDS OK 4 GUNS INSIDE 10 OUT. I tore off the strip of tape and pressed it firmly to Cisco's collar, fluffing out his fur to cover it. I couldn't look into his eyes when I did that, but he panted his happy pant and grinned at me. As far as he was concerned, this was just another adventure, and as long as we were together all was right in his world. As long as we were together.

I had barely finished when the gunman shouted, "Hey! Time's up!"

"Okay, okay!"

I flushed the toilet and emerged from the stall with my throat dry and my palms sweaty. "Can I wash my hands?" I asked.

"No." He gestured toward the main hall. "Get back in there."

He just wanted to refuse me a favor. That was why I had asked.

I said, "What about my dog?"

"What about him?"

"He needs to pee. Come on," I added quickly, before he could respond, "please? He's just a dog. He doesn't understand. It'll only take a minute. Please? Here, you can take him." I thrust the leash at him, knowing he wouldn't take it because doing so would mean lowering his rifle. "I don't even have to go with him. Please?"

He hesitated, then strode the few feet across the hall to the back door. He pushed it open, said something to the soldier who was standing there, and then jerked his head toward me. "Make it snappy," he said.

Training your dog to toilet on command can save time at dog shows and save misery on cold wet mornings when you're standing in your slippers on the other end of the leash wishing your dog would hurry up. I never imagined that it might also one day save my life. I edged between the two soldiers with my heart pounding and went down the shallow steps that led from the covered porch to the expanse of open lawn that faced the path leading to the lake. On the other side of the building was the fenced exercise yard where the kids took their dogs to potty, but the soldiers didn't know that. It was precisely to avoid the fence that I wanted to take Cisco out through this door.

I knew they wouldn't let us go far, so I didn't try. I walked a dozen feet away and told Cisco, "Okay, potty." He obligingly lifted his leg on a small bush. With my back to the soldier on the porch, I unzipped my pouch and took out the sock that was still there from yesterday. The sock that would retain great memories of a long romp and jerky treats at the end. The sock that, I hoped, was still infused with scent. I offered it to Cisco and said quietly, "Cisco, track."

"Hey." The voice came sharply from the porch. "What are you doing?"

I didn't turn around. "He always gets to play with his toy when he's finished."

"That's stupid." Thunder rolled. "Get back in here."

"Okay, I'm coming."

I dropped the sock on the ground and knelt as though to pick it up. Cisco sniffed enthusiastically. I put one hand on his neck, as though petting him, and with the other I brushed the grass with my fingers. "Cisco, track," I said into his ear, and when I did I unclipped his leash.

The soldier shouted, "Now!"

"Okay!" I stood up and turned, still holding the leash and pretending not to notice that my good, sweet, obedient dog was galloping off in the other direction, tail waving, nose drinking in the richly scented air, heading toward the lake.

"Hey!" the soldier shouted, and took a step toward me. His gun tracked Cisco.

"What?"

I then looked down and pretended to notice for the first time that my dog was gone. I stared in pretend dismay at the stretched-out O-ring I had removed from Cisco's Therapy Dog tag in the restroom, now attached to the leash clip and making it appear as though it had simply come loose from his collar. I spun around but all I could see of my good, brave dog was his tail, spinning for

balance, as he ran down the hill. *Go, Cisco. Run...*
*Run...*

But when I turned back to the soldier and held
up the empty leash, my tears were not pretend.

# CHAPTER TWENTY-FOUR

The militants had blocked access to the camp a quarter of a mile away by two vehicles parked nose to nose across the road. Each one was wired with a clearly visible explosive device designed to detonate when the wheels rotated. The bomb disposal unit was on its way. If ever there had been a doubt about Buck's theory, there was no longer.

Five hundred yards behind the blockade, a command post of sorts was set up. Fire and Rescue were there, along with every squad car in Hanover County. State police, FBI vans and support units were still arriving. Buck stood near the front of the blockade with Manahan and two other agents, a topographic map spread open on the hood of his car.

"There's a logging road that goes all around the camp," he said, tracing it with his finger. "Accessible by off-road vehicles to a point but it narrows here, and here. You'll only get a three-wheeler or a horse through. Four buildings in a cluster, here, and five small cabins here along the stream. Two open air pavilions. All the elevation is on their side." Which meant that, even if they could get snipers in, there would be no easy vantage point from which they could site their targets. And that the insurgents would be able to see them coming from any direction. "I checked with the Forest Service. They've got two choppers in the air that can be over our location in five minutes."

"No," Manahan said. "We're not going to give away our position until we know what we're dealing with. These people are known to be trigger happy."

"What about robots?"

"We've got drones on the way. They're an hour and a half out."

Buck stared at him. "That's too long."

Manahan was grim. "You're not in the most accessible area geographically, Sheriff. That may be one reason this area was targeted. Once an adversary inserts itself and takes control, they know that help will be a long time coming."

Buck drew a breath and turned back to the map. "You could send a recon team on foot around the lake and come in from the west. There's wooded cover the whole way. It's going to take a while, but it's the safest way."

Manahan nodded. "I'll need a couple of men who know the terrain."

"You've got them."

Manahan said, "Sheriff." He paused and Buck looked up. "There's something else you should know. Our last piece of intelligence from Brunner indicated that one of the cell members might be from the law enforcement community. How confident are you in the security of your department?"

Buck stared at him. "Confident."

"You've never had a leak?"

"Besides the one you sent me?"

"Good enough." Manahan's nod was terse. "How many kids are we talking about?"

"I don't have that number." Buck looked around. "Wyn…"

"I'll call the office for the permit," she said, and started to turn away.

A hoarse voice near Buck's shoulder said, "Twenty-five."

Buck looked around and saw Miles Young. His face was white and strained and his eyes reflected the kind of horrified disbelief that only the shock of a scene such as this could generate: the quiet mountain road crisscrossed by fire trucks, police cars, crime scene vans and men in body armor. But he held Buck's gaze steadily and he said, "Twenty-five children and dogs, four instructors, three counselors, a nurse, a cook and a vet tech."

The deputy next to Miles said, "I'm sorry, Sheriff, he insisted I let him through. He said he knew you."

Manahan turned to one of the agents. "I want a list of everybody at that camp, particularly the children, with backgrounds."

"On it."

Miles said, "I got a call from the security company. I couldn't reach Raine or the camp office. I called the police but all they said was that they were investigating."

"And that's exactly what we're doing," Buck said tersely, and turned back to the map.

"What is it?" Miles demanded quietly. "What do you need?"

"We don't know yet," Buck said. "There may have been some kind of incident at the camp."

Miles said, "What kind of incident?"

Buck did not want to think about what kind of incident. The kind of incident that screamed out of the headlines and scarred the heart of a nation for years, for decades. The kind of incident in which everything changed on a single breath. The kind of incident from which no one who was involved ever, ever recovered.

Buck repeated tightly, "We don't know."

Miles said, "I have resources. I might be able to get things done quicker than you can. If you—"

"Look, Young," Buck interrupted shortly, "you shouldn't be here. I know you're worried, but the best way you can help is by staying out of the way. I may have already lost a deputy up there and you can be damn sure I'm not going to lose Raine too. So go on home. She's my wife, not yours."

Around him radios continued to crackle and engines idled, voices buzzed and feet ran. But all Buck heard was the echo of his own words. And all he saw was the way the back of Wyn's shoulders stiffened just before she walked away.

Miles Young said coldly, "My *daughter* is in there."

With a shaft of pain that was almost visible, Buck tore his gaze away from Wyn's retreating figure, but not before he saw her slip something off her finger and drop it into her pocket. He looked back at Miles, whose face was filled with a mixture of fury and contempt. Buck said stiffly, "I'm sorry. I didn't know about your daughter. But you can't be here."

He turned back to the map as one of the agents said, "Mr. Young, maybe you can answer some questions for us. Do you mind walking back to my car with me so we can talk?"

And it was just about then that the skies opened up and the deluge came.

The rain roared on the metal roof of the building, drowning out the barking of the dogs. I rested my cheek on my updrawn knees and tried not to cry. The rain would have destroyed the scent. Cisco had no chance of finding Gene Hicks again. And even if he could somehow do it, what made me think Hicks was still there? And even if he was, that he would see the message, or understand it, or want to help us if he could? He was homeless. He didn't even have a phone. It had been a stupid idea.

There might be guards around the lake. One of them might have seen Cisco running loose and shot him, or caught him and locked him up. At best, Cisco was wandering through the storm, lost and alone. At worst, I would never see him again. Ever.

I felt a punch on my shoulder. I looked up.

237

Jolene looked parched and feverish, and her eyes were bright. She said hoarsely, "Hey. You had to try."

I nodded, but it was scant comfort.

The rain pounded. Neither of us said anything for a long time.

I glanced over at her. "My first dog," I said, with difficulty, "I mean my first working dog—she was amazing. Her name was Cassidy. She taught me everything I know about dogs, about search and rescue, about life, really. I can't tell you how many saves we made together. We were so in sync I didn't even have to tell her what to do, she just did it. Working with her was like poetry. Like dancing. We were inseparable for almost fourteen years. When people would call me a dog lover, I would always say, No. I love *a* dog. I always thought there would never be another dog like her. And I was right."

To my surprise, Jolene actually glanced at me. Until then I wasn't sure she was listening, or even interested.

"When she died it was like she took a piece of me with her. In a way she did. She took a piece of my life—all those years we'd lived through together, the things we'd accomplished, the memories we made. Gone. And the scar she left on my heart was so hard and so thick that for the longest time there was no way for another dog to get in. I didn't *want* another dog to get in, because it's a lot harder to open up your heart than to keep it closed, if you know what I mean, and I just couldn't. I didn't have that kind of courage. Even when I got Cisco, it wasn't the same. I could never love another dog like I loved Cassidy. But after a while...I don't know. He wasn't Cassidy, and I didn't love him the same, but that was okay. It was good, even. In some ways what I have with Cisco is better than it was with Cassidy, and I never thought that would happen. But I think maybe that's the whole point with dogs. They keep giving us chances, you know—to be better, to grow bigger, to love more. But we have to give them a chance first."

Jolene said nothing. I hadn't expected her to. I rested my head on my knees again and listened to the rain.

After a long time Jolene spoke. "I think your dog's okay," she said. "We would've heard a shot if he wasn't."

Scant comfort, maybe. But at least she made the effort.

And then she frowned. "There's something strange about this whole setup."

I could barely hear her over the rain and thought I had misunderstood. "What?"

She said, "It's been over four hours. Nothing is happening. They're not making any demands. They're not trying to scare us with their power. They're not threatening us or mistreating us. They're not even preparing for a siege. They're just...keeping us here. Like they're waiting for something."

I found that thought more frightening than any other possibility I'd considered. "Waiting for what?"

She winced in pain as she shook her head. "I don't know." She blew out a breath and leaned her head back against the wall again, closing her eyes. "I can't think. But whatever it is, it'd better be soon." She opened her eyes briefly. "So far it's been a peaceful takeover. But that won't last. It never does. So...it'd better be soon."

The brief downpour gave cover for the advance team, but it also slowed them down considerably. By the landmarks described in the last radio check-in, they were still twenty minutes away from visual contact.

That was too long.

"We need to call in the helicopters," Buck said tensely. "At least we can get pictures. You can drop a SWAT team in."

Manahan ignored him.

Buck strode back to his car and pulled on his flak vest. The rain had left the day dark and steamy, with a ground fog wisping through the woods on either side of the road and leaves dripping in an early twilight. The weather wasn't over, and the going wouldn't get any easier. He slammed the car door, opened the trunk, took out his rifle. He started back toward the blockade.

Manahan said, "Sheriff, you are not authorized for this."

Buck said, "This is my county. The safety of every soul in it is my responsibility. That makes me authorized."

Behind him, Buck heard other car doors slam. One by one his deputies came to stand behind him. Out of the corner of his eye, Buck noted that Wyn was one of them.

The patient expression Manahan tried to adapt did not disguise the steel in his eyes. He said, "Sheriff, I appreciate the help you've given us so far, but know that I will do whatever I have to to make sure the lives of those children are not endangered by a hothead with a hero complex. We have choppers standing by. When I call for them they'll be here in five minutes. Until then, we follow procedure."

Buck said angrily, "What makes you think that by the time you get finished following procedure there'll be anybody left alive to endanger? You know as well as I do that if this was a hostage situation they would've tried to make contact by now! The chances are—"

But then he saw Miles Young, who had been leaning against a car a few feet away, straighten up. He saw the look on his face. And he said nothing more.

Manahan repeated, "We follow procedure." He turned away.

Buck started to move forward but Miles Young said in an odd, still tone, "Sheriff." Buck realized that the other man was no longer looking at him, but peering fixedly at a space over his left shoulder. Buck heard the sound of movement in the brush behind him and he spun around, rifle at the ready.

"Halt! Police!" he shouted. "Identify yourself!"

A dozen weapons were pulled and aimed; a dozen officers and agents swung into position as the clear form of a man appeared from the wet shadows of the woods. "Don't shoot!" he called. "I'm unarmed."

And that was when a golden retriever appeared in the mist beside him, tongue lolling, tail wagging, and trotted affably toward them.

# CHAPTER TWENTY-FIVE

"I'm not a part of this!" Buck had Reggie Connor on his face in the road, roughly cuffing his hands behind his back. "I'm turning myself in, but I want immunity, I'm telling you! I'm not a part of this!"

Buck jerked Reggie to his feet, sweating and breathing hard. "What are you not a part of, you stupid son of a bitch? Where are they? What have they done to the kids?"

Reggie was soaked and muddy and looked terrified enough to be telling the truth. "I don't know! They burned up my dad's car! They told me they were going to borrow it and then they burned the damn thing up! I don't need no part of this. I didn't sign up for this!"

"The camp!" Manahan spoke sharply. "What do you know about the camp?"

"Nothing, that's what I'm telling you. I didn't know what they were planning. It was the dog. It wasn't until the dog that I figured it out. And that's when I knew I couldn't have no part in this! I'm turning myself in, but I want a lawyer!"

Miles Young was kneeling on the ground, one arm around a wet and bedraggled Cisco, who looked less relaxed to be here than he had a moment ago. Buck swung his head toward Cisco. "What about the dog?" he demanded.

"It's his collar," Reggie said. "There's writing on it."

Before Buck could make the two strides to Cisco, Miles had pulled off his collar and read the message there. His face sagged with relief as he handed the collar to Buck. "They're alive," he said.

In less than five minutes, the plan was in action. The SWAT team was mobilized to access the building by foot; a phalanx of men was organized to surround the camp on the lake road. "This is a silent approach," Manahan ordered. "You will reconnoiter with the advance team and make no aggressive moves until our intelligence is confirmed. It's reasonable to expect the approach may be mined. These people have already shown they have access to sophisticated munitions. It is imperative that you maintain cover. Sheriff, stand by to—"

Suddenly the air was rent by the screech of a police siren. The blast lasted barely more than a second but it seemed to go on half a lifetime and it was loud enough to be heard two states away. When Buck whipped around, eyes searching the controlled chaos that surrounded him, he saw Lyle Reston, looking stricken and horrified, with one arm inside his squad car. He straightened up slowly and into the frozen silence stammered, "Sheriff, I'm sorry. I...I was reaching for my radio and I accidently..."

Buck just stared at him.

"That's it," Manahan said grimly. "They know where we are now." Then, loudly, "Move in, men, full assault mode! Backup teams, stand ready!"

Buck walked to Reston, who looked increasingly uncomfortable. "Sheriff," he said, "it was an accident."

Buck demanded quietly, "What were you doing on this side of the county this morning? You were supposed to be patrolling in town."

A quick shift of his gaze. "You're right. But I had a tip on Connor's whereabouts and I decided to follow up. It paid off, too, didn't it?"

"Oh yeah?" Buck walked around the unit and opened the trunk. "What kind of tip?"

His answer wasn't quite fast enough. "One of the neighbors. He called about the car."

Buck came around the car, a handkerchief wrapped around the hand grip of a .44 Magnum. He said, "When we find the bullet that killed Willie Banks, will ballistics match it to this gun?"

Lyle went very still.

"One day we're going to have a long talk about this," Buck said. "But right now I don't care why, or how, or what went wrong. What I care about is twenty-five kids and how you're going to help us get them back to their mamas and daddies. Hand over your service weapon."

There was an instant when panic shot through Lyle's eyes and he looked as though he might do something foolish. The pressure of steel in his ribs stopped him. Wyn said, "Do it."

She had always had Buck's back.

But even as he was disarmed and cuffed, even as his fellow officers stared at him in confusion and contempt, all Lyle returned was a pitying look. "It doesn't matter," he said. "It's over. You're too late."


I was starving. It was past the dogs' dinnertime, and the children's too. The kids were cranky. Some of them started crying again, and begging to call their moms and dads. When Margie stood up to go comfort them, a soldier swung his gun at her. Some of the dogs—particularly the spoiled ones like Pepper and Mischief—sat and barked sharply, demanding their dinner. Others chewed or pawed at the bars of their cages.

Steve muttered, "We have to do something. We can't just sit here."

"Who does this?" whispered Kathy, the nurse. "Who takes a camp full of children and dogs hostage? It's crazy!"

"No one is coming for us," said Counselor Bill. "No one knows we're here."

"They know." Jolene's voice was firm, although the effort it cost her to speak was visible. Her lips were cracked and her skin was pinched, and the gauze bandage around her hand was stained with blood. She was dehydrated and clearly in pain. "Procedure is to wait for rescue. Do nothing to provoke the aggressors."

"Hey!" one of the soldiers barked, turning his rifle on her. "Shut up!"

They had never ordered us not to talk before. The strain was starting to show on them too.

And then the soldier swung the rifle toward Margie. "Quiet those kids down!" And to me, "And the dogs! Shut them up!"

I said, very calmly, "I don't have any more treats. They're hungry and thirsty and they've been crated too long. There's nothing I can do." I thought to myself, *He's losing it.* And my heart started to pound.

Margie slowly pushed herself to her feet. Her hair was greasy and tangled with sweat and her makeup had long since worn off, but her eyes were defiant and unafraid. She called across the room to the row of children, "Hey, kids! We're going to have a sing along! Who remembers our camp song?"

Only the sound of barking and an occasional sob broke the silence. Margie began to sing,

*Oh beautiful, for collie dogs...*

She said, "Come on, kids, you know it! Where are my stars?" She began again:

*Oh beautiful, for collie dogs...*

Another voice, small but true, joined in.

*And German shepherds too...*

When I looked, Melanie was on her feet. I gave her the biggest smile I could find, even as my eyes flooded with tears. One by one other voices joined, and other children stood, until the sound of their singing almost drowned out the barking of the dogs.

*For poodles and Siberians*
*With shining eyes of blue!*
*Oh Labradors, oh Rottweilers...*

That was when we heard the police siren.

For a moment nothing happened. The singing voices trickled off, the dogs continued to bark, and some to howl. It was only one sweet sharp blast of hope, over as abruptly as it had begun, but it froze our world for a moment; it changed everything. No one blinked, no one breathed. For a moment I think we weren't entirely sure of what we had heard.

And then, movement. The radios on the collars of the soldiers started to crackle. They spoke words into them that I could neither hear nor comprehend. I looked at Jolene. Her nostrils were flared, her expression still and alert. The soldiers started to move toward the doors, backing away, covering us with their rifles. And then they were gone.

For a moment we just stared at each other. Someone whispered, "Is that it? Are they gone?"

Melanie launched herself across the room into my arms and I swept her up, hugging her harder than I've ever hugged anyone in my life. The other kids started to swarm into the arms of the instructors and counselors, their protectors. Steve ran toward the nearest door until Jolene shouted, "No! Stay away from the doors!" And he had the good sense to listen to her.

She made us all move away from the walls and doors to the center of the room, near the dogs, and we huddled there, I don't know how long. We watched the doors. We clung to each other. We waited. And then we heard the sound of helicopters overhead, lots of them, close. My face broke into a broad grin as I turned my face toward the ceiling, and so did Steve's and Margie's and Kathy's and Lee's. Melanie looked up at me anxiously. "Is it over?"

And then I heard the sweetest words I had ever heard in my life. "FBI! Stand back!"

I hugged Melanie tightly. "Yeah," I said. "It's over."

# CHAPTER TWENTY-SIX

Sunday night. We were all curled up together on Miles's big sofa, a bowl of popcorn between us, watching *Independence Day* on his giant-screen television. Pepper slept next to Melanie and Cisco was stretched out on the sofa next to me, his head in my lap. I did not like to encourage him to get on the furniture, but Miles had no scruples whatsoever. And besides, this was a special occasion.

Mischief and Magic, the clowns, lolled belly-up on the plush rug in front of the television. Nike, mine for the weekend, had dutifully explored every inch of the double-wide for danger, and had eventually settled in a corner where she could keep an eye on everything: Miles, me, Melanie, the dogs, the television. The way she lay so alertly in sphinx position with her gaze straight ahead made it look as though she was actually enjoying the movie.

Melanie fell asleep before the White House blew up, her head on her dad's shoulder, one hand in the popcorn bowl and the other entangled in Pepper's fur. I woke up with a start around the time Will Smith was dragging the alien across the desert by the tentacles. Miles soothed me with a kiss atop my head. "Okay?" he whispered.

I nodded and settled against his shoulder again, stroking Cisco's ear.

So much about the past twenty-four hours was a blur, and was likely to remain so. I remember Melanie running into her father's arms, and I remember the look on his face as he swept her up, but I do not remember how we got out of the building. I remember Cisco galloping to me, all grins and waving tail, and I remember falling to my knees and sobbing out loud as I wrapped my arms around him. I remember Miles kissing me and holding my face with strong fingers curved against my scalp and whispering, "I love your hair!" which made me laugh and cry even harder.

Someone told me that two of the insurgents had been shot trying to escape. I don't know who they were. Someone else—I don't know who—told me about Reggie Connor and how Cisco had found him and how he turned out to be in collusion with the militants the whole time, but none of it made much sense to me. I remember thinking, dazed, that it must have been Reggie's sock Cisco had found by the lake after all, and that poor Gene Hicks, a bit player in this whole drama, had probably moved on long before any of this ever happened.

What made even less sense to me was Lyle Reston. I had known him since he was six.

They took Jolene to the hospital, where I heard she had surgery on her hand but was doing fine and would be released on Monday. Nike came home with me.

I hadn't had much sleep. The FBI interviews had lasted until midnight, and then I stayed to help Margie and Steve with the hysterical parents who came to pick up their children. Somehow I ended up at Miles's house with all the dogs. He made me something wonderful to eat. I slept.

The FBI was still combing the woods with special search teams and helicopters, but I had a feeling they wouldn't find any more of the terrorists. This had been too well planned.

It would take weeks, if then, for all the details to be sorted out, but the prevailing theory was that Camp Bluebird had been used as a training site and munitions dump for the radicals, just as I'd guessed. The arrival of a camp filled with children and dogs had been an inconvenience for them, to say the least, and the addition of an explosives dog demo pushed the situation to critical. When Jolene arrived early and Willie knew he couldn't finish moving all the munitions before Nike discovered them, he decided to go rogue, figuring he had a better chance at survival by trying to sell the stolen munitions himself than to face the charges that would be levied if he was discovered to be working for the militants. Lyle Reston claimed he carried out the orders of a man called the Professor when he shot Willie. He still denied the murder of Carl Brunner, but a ballistics test of the bullet found deep in the frame of Jessie Connor's burned out car told a different story.

By the way, when I asked Jolene just before they put her in the ambulance why she had decided to come out to the camp two hours early, she gave me what in other circumstances might have passed for a wry grin and replied, "Just to piss you off."

Reggie maintained that his involvement was only peripheral, and that he knew he was in over his head when they burned up his dad's car. He continued to insist he knew nothing about the hostage event, but speculated that they might have been planning to negotiate for the return of the munitions that had been confiscated from Willie's pickup. Beyond that, the last I heard, he refused to give up names or say more, hoping for a lawyer who could cut him a deal for immunity. Good luck with that.

Henry Middleton was being interviewed, but so far could be charged with nothing more than exercising his right to freedom of assembly. He claimed absolutely no knowledge of the activities of any of the suspects in the case, and was so arrogant he didn't even ask for a lawyer. The FBI was no easily discouraged, however, and I had a feeling he'd be asking for one soon.

The scary thing was that the FBI never found the hand grenades or the remainder of the ammunition that Nike had discovered buried in the rocks. Or at least they hadn't so far. The terrorists had not left empty-handed.

"I can't believe that idiot is still coming here tomorrow," Miles said, stirring me from a troubled half-doze. I opened my eyes to see one of Jeb

Wilson's campaign ads on television. "Some kind of crazy machismo BS, I guess. Everybody wants to be a hero on the Fourth of July."

I blinked a couple of times to focus and reached for a handful of popcorn. "I don't think he's going to be in the parade anymore. Just make a quick speech afterward."

"And that's the other thing. Why are they still having the parade?"

"There's no reason not to. The problem is all way on the other side of the county, and it's not even a problem anymore. Most people probably don't know what happened yet. Besides, everything turned out okay." I popped a piece of popcorn in my mouth, and glanced up at him. "You never did tell me what you've got against Jeb Wilson."

He hesitated. "I've had a couple of run-ins with him during the course of doing business that turned out to be not entirely above-board. Almost lost my shirt in one, and he had a very creative way of keeping me from filing a complaint. But it's not just one thing. It's a pattern. He was on the board of one of the banks that got nailed in the sub-prime lending scandal...only by the time the bank collapsed he was no longer on the board and his record was squeaky clean. Then there was that insurance debacle in Florida after the hurricane, and his company wasn't even indicted."

I said, "Those sound like the kinds of things that could ruin a campaign."

He shrugged and took a handful of popcorn. "For an ordinary person, maybe. But Wilson's got a hell of a cleanup team. Every time the opposition tries to nail him, the evidence mysteriously gets turned against them. And the scary thing is, if he makes it to Washington, there's no limit to the kind of damage he could do."

I wondered if Buck knew about any of this. And then I figured he had more important things on his mind right now.

I said, "So I take it you're not going to the parade."

He replied without hesitation. "I am not. I'm staying right here with my two girls and barbecuing hamburgers and watching fireworks from my deck."

I snuggled closer. "Um, one of your girls has to take Nike back to her owner at nine in the morning."

Miles tilted my face up with his finger and kissed me. "And I'm driving you," he said. "Barbecue starts at one."

I rested my head against his shoulder and closed my eyes. Sometimes a little overprotectiveness is not such a bad thing.

The one thing that never ceases to amaze me is the resilience of dogs and kids. At nine the next morning, we drove into town with Pepper and Cisco happily looking out the windows of Miles's SUV while Melanie, sitting between them, chatted on about her adventures at dog camp. In honor of the holiday,

Melanie had tied festive red-white-and-blue bandan-nas around the golden retrievers' necks and had wanted to do the same for Nike until I convinced her that working dogs didn't dress up for holidays. Nike, good police dog that she was, was crated quietly in the cargo area of the SUV for the short trip into town. Since she had come home with me, she had been nothing but alert and obedient, her intense gaze taking in every corner, crevice, shadow and nuance of her new environment. I thought she was looking for Jolene.

"The bad thing about it is," Melanie went on, "we never got to do the play. Or have the competitions on Sunday. I think Pepper could have won Idol."

My smile was a little strained only because even thinking about the camp, about what should have been, what never would be, and what might have happened still made me a little nauseous. It was kind of like the way you feel after stepping off a really scary roller coaster, thinking you're okay, right before your knees buckle. Miles noticed and covered my hand with his briefly.

I said, "I guess Margie will be refunding a lot of tuition."

"I don't think anyone will be asking for it," Miles replied. "We got our kids back. You guys kept them safe. Who's going to put a price on that?"

Melanie said, "You know what would be fun? We could have an agility trial before lunch and Dad could be the judge. Mischief and Magic can't be in it though," she added quickly. "They're too fast."

This time the smile was more genuine; almost a grin. "Cisco is pretty fast."

"True," she agreed sagely, "but he lacks discipline. You're always saying so."

Miles suppressed a chuckle as he made the turn into Courthouse Square and found a parking place. It was all decorated for the parade with swags of red and white bunting draped from the white columns of the courthouse, waving in the breeze from the reviewing stand set up in front of the big building, and continuing around on both sides to the public safety building and the jail. Huge American flags waved from the east and west corners of the square, as well as from the center of the courthouse portico, and bleachers were set up in front of the reviewing stand. In contrast to the past twenty-four hours, it all seemed surreal; garish and overdone. I felt that wave of vertigo again, a touch of queasiness in my core.

"Wow." Melanie looked around appreciatively. "Pretty cool. Maybe we should stay for the parade after all." And without waiting for a response, she reached for her door handle. "I'll go in with you, Raine. You'll probably need some help."

I said, "I don't think so." Even as Miles reached his arm over the seat to stop her and added, "Whoa, kiddo."

I had offered to bring Nike to the hospital, or even to return her to Jolene at home, but Jolene was still a by-the-book kind of girl. Nike was property of the sheriff's department; she wanted her returned to the sheriff's department. And given everything that was going on there now, the sheriff's department was definitely not the place for a little girl. I wasn't even sure it was the place for a big girl, and I didn't intend to spend any more time inside than necessary.

I gave Melanie an apologetic smile as I got out. "Sorry, official business," I said. To Miles I added, "I'll just be a minute."

Cisco suddenly sat up straight and barked out the window. Melanie twisted around to see what he was barking at. "Hey," she said, frowning. "It's that creepy guy from the woods."

Miles frowned. "Do you mean the one with the gun?"

Startled, I followed the direction of her gaze. "Oh my goodness, you're right." The man who stood in the shade of the big poplar that marked the entrance to the park across the street from us was wearing camo pants, a green cotton hunter's vest and combat boots. When Cisco barked, he turned to look at us. It was definitely Gene Hicks, but there was something different about him. I couldn't put my finger on what it was. "How weird is that?" He had mentioned something about trying to sell fireworks in town, so maybe that was why he was here. Maybe the FBI swarming all over the woods had driven him out of his campsite. It just seemed so strange to see him here.

Miles got out of the car and came to stand beside me. Why do men do that? Like their mere presence could frighten off imaginary threats. I gave him a disparaging look and deliberately raised my arm, waving to the man across the street. He looked at me for a moment with no expression whatsoever. Then he smiled, took an apple from the oversized pocket of his vest, and saluted me with it. He walked away with an easy, sauntering gait, munching the apple.

"Creepy," muttered Miles.

I frowned. "He is not." But what was it that was different? What was bothering me?

Melanie said, "Well, I didn't like him. He had a snake tattooed on his hand. He was scarier than the soldiers."

Miles gave me an "I told you so" look and I ignored him, walking around the vehicle to open the cargo door of the SUV. The minute I did, Nike became agitated. She stood up in her crate and barked, pawing at the wire, even grabbing it with her teeth as though she was trying to chew her way through. Did she know Jolene was here? Did she recognize the place she had only worked in for four days? Whatever it was, the sight of that big police dog trying to chew her way through the wire cage was disconcerting, and of course her barking got Pepper and Cisco started. There was no way I was going to try to handle her by myself. I closed the back door of the SUV and called "Sorry!" to Miles over the sound of barking dogs. "Be right back!"

I crossed the parking lot and went quickly around the walkway to the sheriff's department, still wondering what it was about Gene Hicks that was different, and wishing I'd had a chance to talk to him.

I pushed open the sheriff's department door, and for the first time in all the years I'd been coming here I couldn't wait to leave. Even before I opened the door I could feel the urgency and the dread; I could smell the sweat of overworked, over-dedicated officers and the shock of betrayal that permeated every stone and tile. It brought it all back. It reminded me it wasn't over. It made me want to go home and play with my dogs and barbecue hamburgers and pretend the past weekend had never happened.

Annabelle looked at me with big eyes and a harried expression when I came in. "Hey, Raine. You okay? None of us can believe this. Just awful, isn't it? I'm glad you're okay."

I'm sure I said something nice to her but I really just wanted to do what I'd come to do and go home. I spotted Jolene in the bullpen and started toward her. It was odd to see her in civilian clothes—a white shirt and jeans—and her arm was compressed against her chest in a dark blue sling. The bruise around her eye was still purple, and the eye itself was bloodshot, but the swelling had gone down and she looked pretty good for someone who had only gotten out of the hospital a couple of hours ago. Certainly she looked a hundred times better than she had the last time I'd seen her.

The bullpen was crowded and noisy and had that same sour smell of fatigue and nervous energy that clung to the rest of the building. The big white-boards had pictures of faces I didn't know on them, and most alarmingly, faces that I did know: Lyle Reston, Reggie Connor, Henry Middleton. More than once I saw pictures of the old-fashioned yellow "Don't Tread on Me" flag with the coiled rattlesnake. I could feel eyes follow me as I passed. I tried to smile, tried to look brave. I wanted them to know everything was okay now. It could have gone so much worse, but thanks to them it had not. Everything was okay now. And so I made myself smile.

Jolene got up from her desk as I approached, and for a moment we just looked at each other warily, uncomfortably. I had heard somewhere that when people survive a trauma together—an airplane crash, say, or a shipwreck or a hostage situation—an indelible bond forms between them that no one else will ever understand. I did not think that was going to be the case with Jolene and me.

"Hey," I said, a little awkwardly. "Nike's in the car. She's a little agitated. I thought you'd want to bring her in yourself."

Jolene responded grumpily, "You probably fed her popcorn and talked baby-talk to her."

I scowled briefly. "I did not." In fact, she had shown no interest whatsoever in the popcorn.

Jolene returned my scowl. "I guess I should thank you for keeping her. I would've stopped by your place to pick her up, but the sheriff wanted to see me."

I glanced around, just wanting to be out of here. Everything about this place, and about Jolene in particular, was like reopening a wound, and it disturbed me to think it might always be that way. "I'm sure you would have been excused," I said, trying to be polite. "Aren't you on medical leave?"

Her expression was a little grim. "You only get leave if you're still employed. I'm not sure I am." She lifted a shoulder in a curt dismissive gesture that seemed to carry an undertone of frustration. "It's probably just as well," she said gruffly. "I screwed everything up out there. What kind of cop can't handle the duty in a hick town like this? I deserve to be fired."

That was probably my cue to say something reassuring—which she would have resented—or to agree with her, which would have started a fight and, come to think of it, was probably what she was going for. But to tell the truth, I was barely listening. I couldn't stop looking around the room, trying to figure out what was still nagging at the back of my mind. "What's the deal with all the snake flags?"

"It's the Gadsden Flag," she corrected me with a tone that implied any idiot would know that. "The militants use it as their insignia. Of course, so do the Navy Seals and a lot of other legitimate patriotic organizations, but we're supposed to keep an eye out for it. You know, bumper stickers, tee shirts—"

"Tattoos," I said softly. Something cold was starting to close in around my stomach as bits and scraps of memory started to swarm together like iron shavings drawn to a magnet. Lost homes, unpaid insurance claims, a box of fire crackers that were too big to be fire crackers...

*You can't trust anybody,* Gene Hicks had said, *Not the government, not the banker, not the preacher, not your wife. Not anybody.*

"Yeah, I guess," said Jolene. Then she looked at me sharply. "Do you know somebody with a tattoo like that?"

I said softly, still thinking hard, "Yeah, I do. There was this camper in the woods..."

A green backpack, a green canvas bag filled with grenades. Jeb Wilson. Florida. What was it Miles had said about an insurance debacle after the hurricane? *If he makes it to Washington, there's no limit to the damage he could do...*

The backpack...

*You can't trust anybody,* he'd said. *There's some bad types around...*

That was what was wrong about Gene Hicks. That was what was missing. A hiker without his backpack. Without his gun, without his tent, without his provisions...without his backpack.

My breath left my lungs with a whoosh and I turned to Jolene urgently. "It wasn't us!" I gasped. "It was never about us, don't you see?"

Jolene's brows drew together suspiciously. I must have looked, and sounded, crazy. "What are you talking about?"

"He had firecrackers." My heart was pounding as though I'd just run up a flight of stairs and I could hardly get the words out. "The man in the woods, only I don't think they were firecrackers at all, I think they were some kind of bomb...he practically *told* me what he was planning! Florida, the insurance, the banks…"

Jolene said in a tone that was very quiet and still, "What? What was he planning?"

I looked around the room wildly, although I'm not entirely sure what I was looking for. "Jeb Wilson!" I cried. "The FBI, the state police, every deputy in the county—they were all at the camp and no one was guarding the town! That was what they wanted ! 'When your government goes up in flames'…that's what he said, don't you remember? This was their plan all along!"

The deputies around me had stopped talking, and turned their heads to me, their expressions tense and worried. Buck must have heard me from his office because he came out, looking older and more tired than I ever imagined he could be. He said, "Raine? What's going on?"

But I spared him barely a glance, and turned back to Jolene, desperate to make her understand. She was there, she would know, she *had* to know I was right, she had to believe me. My breath came so rapidly that I thought I might pass out. "'*This is not our mission.*' That's what they kept saying. That's why the FBI can't find them—they had already planned their escape route!"

Buck said, "Raine?"

"He had a backpack," I said tensely, lowly to Jolene. My hands were balled into fists at my sides as I tried to will my thoughts into her mind. "When I saw him in the woods he had a green backpack, and just now—he didn't!"

Her eyes were locked on mine with an intensity that I have never felt from another human being. And it was the weirdest thing, I *felt* her understanding. No one who had not been there would have believed me. No one who had not endured those terrifying hours by my side would have trusted me or even tried to make sense of my hysterical ramblings. But it was as though she looked inside my head and she knew exactly what I was trying to say and she believed me.

The lines around Jolene's mouth grew very tight. "I need my dog," she said.

She shouldered past me, moving in long strides for the door. Before she reached it, she was running. So was I.

# CHAPTER TWENTY-SEVEN

The first bomb Nike alerted to was beneath the reviewing stand. The square was evacuated within minutes; the entire town was sealed off within the hour. There were two more bombs, each with enough fire power to take out half a block. One was in the courthouse, the other beneath the jail. They don't leave witnesses.

But this time their mission failed. This time the bomb squad was on site in fifteen minutes. The entire town was declared secure by sundown. There was no parade that Fourth of July, no fireworks, no picnics on the town square. But it was still the best Independence Day in recent memory. Because this time the good guys won.

Jeb Wilson held a press conference in which he praised the hard work and ingenuity of the Hanover County Sheriff's Department, operating under the inspired leadership of Buck Lawson. It was carried on the national news, and Buck's picture was in every newspaper in the state. A reporter out of Asheville did a feature on the hostage crisis and called it "The Heroes of Camp Bluebird." A big-time news magazine picked it up and Cisco's picture was on the cover. For a while we were pretty famous.

Buck gave Jolene and Nike commendations for actions above and beyond the call of duty, and presented them with medals at a Chamber of Commerce dinner a few weeks later. Practically the whole town was there. Jolene was offered a job with the FBI, and I think she considered it. But in the end she decided to, in her words, "stick around here for a while and see how it goes. After all, it can't get much worse." All things considered, I suppose she was right about that.

Jolene still has a lot to learn about life in a small town, and believe me, she's not the type to take instruction gracefully. But I understand why she decided to stay, and I'm kind of glad. We'll never be best friends, but there might be something to that thing about bonding through trauma after all. I only know that seeing her around town these days doesn't plunge me back into the nightmare any more, like I thought it would. Instead it makes me kind of proud. We survived. And we did it together.

Reggie Connor and Lyle Reston were transferred to federal custody and out of the Hanover County jail. From the description I gave them of Gene Hicks, the FBI was able to identify him as Henry Caleb Jarvis, a forty three year old munitions expert with fifteen years military experience and six other aliases. He was not from Florida, had never been married, had no children. He very likely had never owned a dog. Every one of those details he had given me had been designed to play me, while at the same time present-ing a profile of everything the so-called Patriots were fighting against: corruption, injustice, self-serving politicians. By reviewing thousands of hours of sur-veillance video, the FBI had so far identified him at the sites of ten different bombings, or thwarted bombings, in the past five years. As for their chances of catching him? Modern crime-fighting techniques are pretty good at snagging perpetrators who go through airports and transit stations, who pass by security cameras in retail stores and fast food joints, or who drive their cars through toll booths. But some-one who walks the wooded back trails of America's national forests and parklands? Not so much. I some-times wake up in the middle of the night with my heart pounding, thinking about that. Remembering the way he had petted my dog. Remembering the way he had saluted me with that apple from across the street, knowing that he had planted a bomb not ten feet from where I stood.

"I was so wrong about him," I told Buck that night of the commendations dinner. "I was wrong about everything. Cisco even liked him."

Buck smiled faintly. He looked handsome in his dress uniform, but there were lines about his mouth and his eyes that I was afraid would never go away. He said, "Cisco likes everybody. Not a good measuring stick."

I nodded reluctantly. "It's just...I don't know how I can ever trust my own judgment again. How could I have been so *wrong*?"

Buck glanced down at his glass. The Chamber had sprung for champagne—not a very good champagne that would end up giving me a headache in the morning—but I happened to know Buck was drinking sparkling cider. He was running for office, after all. He said, "If it makes you feel any better, I'm not going to win any prizes for my judgment either. I accused Jolene of being a spy, while the whole time I was the signing the pay check of a murderer who was plotting treason against the United States government. Talk about feeling like an ass."

I said, "Well, Jolene was an easy mistake to make."

The subject under discussion was busy getting her picture taken with her hero dog for the local paper. We glanced their way, and Buck smiled. It seemed like the first genuine smile I'd seen from him in months. And then he sobered. He said, "Truth of the matter is, that's not even the biggest mistake I've made lately." He glanced again at his glass. "Raine, there's something I've been meaning to talk to you about. I wonder if—"

But it was at that moment that Miles came up and slipped his arm around my waist. "You about ready to go, sugar?" he asked. He greeted Buck with, "Nice speech, Sheriff."

Buck nodded in acknowledgment. I thought the atmosphere between them was a bit cooler than it had been in the past, but that might be just me. At any rate, I was glad to go home. I had not wanted to hear whatever Buck had been about to say.

I didn't see much of Buck after that, partly because he had his hands full with the election and everything else that had happened, partly because of something else. I remember how the FBI brought the children out first, and I stayed back to help with the dogs. When I came out, the blocked road had been cleared and the camp lawn was swirling in blue lights, crackling with radio static, crowded with uniforms. Buck had been among those uniforms, and as I came down the steps, he started to push his way toward me, and I remember the expression on his face when Miles swept me up and I clung to him, laughing and crying and holding on to him. Remembering the look in Buck's eyes at that moment wakes me up in the middle of the night, too, because I've recently come to understand some things that are, in many ways, even scarier than those six hours we were held at gunpoint.

I still have nightmares, but oddly enough, not about the soldiers. In my nightmare, I run out of the public safety building and around the walkway and into the parking lot and Jolene gets Nike out of the car, just the way it happened in real life, and I scream to Miles, "Go! Get out of here! Drive! *Go!*" But in my nightmare he just leans against the car, smiling at me kind of sadly, and he doesn't move at all, and I keeping screaming at him because doesn't he realize that everything I love is in that car? Then, in my nightmare, Cisco starts to bark and I realize that the bomb isn't in the courthouse after all; it's in the car. And that's where I wake up.

The experts call that kind of thing a form of post-traumatic stress disorder. Maybe one day I'll talk to Jolene about it. One day.

On a bright Sunday afternoon in August, I drove Miles and Melanie to the Asheville airport, where they would fly to Atlanta and catch a connecting flight to Rio De Janeiro, Brazil. Miles did not, of course, need me to drive him to the airport, but Melanie used it as an excuse to spend more time with Pepper, whom Miles had somehow finagled into the VIP lounge. Pepper would be staying with me while they were gone, and from the length of the care list Melanie gave me, you'd think I had never even seen a dog before, much less taken care of one.

Melanie spent the hour before boarding in protracted good-byes while Miles and I sipped fancy club soda and pretended to watch the game on television. At one point Miles said, "I'm not that comfortable about leaving you," which surprised a laugh out of me.

"Don't worry," I assured him. "I promise not to be taken hostage by any crazed gunmen while you're gone."

"Talk is cheap," he retorted. Then he brought my fingers to his lips for a kiss and said, seriously, "Don't get taken hostage by crazed gunmen while I'm gone."

When their flight was called, Melanie handed me Pepper's leash and knelt to hug her puppy. "It's going to be fine, Pepper. I'll be back before you know it. And you'll have Cisco to look after you."

"And me," I reminded her. I hugged her with my free arm and she hugged me back. There was a little lump in my throat. I was going to miss her. "Have a good time. Call me."

"Every day," she promised.

"Well," I suggested, "maybe every other day."

She grinned and waved at me with her boarding pass as she left for the gate.

Miles waited until the room was empty to kiss me good-bye. Then he leaned his forehead against mine and looked somberly into my eyes. "Take care of yourself. I mean it."

I said, "For heaven's sake, Miles, you're as bad as Melanie. It's only two weeks."

He smiled and kissed me again. "Love you, babe." So easy for him to say.

He swung the strap of his leather carry-on over his shoulder and blew me another kiss as he left the room. I waited until he was gone to whisper, "I love you too, Miles."

And it cost me my heart.

# ALSO IN THE RAINE STOCKTON DOG MYSTERY SERIES

## SMOKY MOUNTAIN TRACKS

*A child has been kidnapped and abandoned in the mountain wilderness. Her only hope is Raine Stockton and her young, untried tracking dog Cisco...*

## RAPID FIRE

*Raine and Cisco are brought in by the FBI to track a terrorist...a terrorist who just happens to be Raine's old boyfriend.*

## GUN SHY

*Raine rescues a traumatized service dog, and soon begins to suspect he is the only witness to a murder.*

## BONE YARD
### A Novella

*Cisco digs up human remains in Raine's back yard, and mayhem ensues. Could this be evidence of a serial killer, a long-unsolved mass murder, or something even more sinister...and closer to home?*

## SILENT NIGHT

*It's Christmastime in Hansonville, N.C., and Raine and Cisco are on the trail of a missing teenager. But when a newborn is abandoned in the manger of the town's living nativity and Raine walks in on what appears to be the scene of a murder, the holidays take a very dark turn for everyone concerned.*

### The Dead Season

*Raine and Cisco take a job leading a wilderness hike for troubled teenagers, and soon find themselves trapped on a mountainside in a blizzard...with a killer.*

### All That Glitters
#### A Holiday Short Story eBook

*Raine looks back on how she and Cisco met and solved their first crime in this Christmas Cozy short story. Sold separately as an e-book or bundled with the print edition of HIGH IN TRIAL.*

### High in Trial

*A carefree weekend turns deadly when Raine and Cisco travel to the South Carolina low country for an agility competition.*

### Double Dog Dare

*Raine and Cisco are invited to an exclusive Caribbean island for a luxury vacation, but trouble finds them even in paradise.*

## SPINE-CHILLING SUSPENSE
## BY DONNA BALL

### SHATTERED

*A missing child, a desperate call for help in the middle of the night…is this a cruel hoax, or the work of a maniacal serial killer who is poised to strike again?*

### NIGHT FLIGHT

*She's an innocent woman who knows too much. Now she's fleeing through the night without a weapon and without a phone, and her only hope for survival is a cop who's willing to risk his badge—and his life—to save her.*

### SANCTUARY

*They came to the peaceful, untouched mountain wilderness of Eastern Tennessee seeking an escape from the madness of modern life. But when they built their luxury homes in the heart of virgin forest they did not realize that something was there before them…something ancient and horrible; something that will make them believe that monsters are real.*

### EXPOSURE

*Everyone has secrets, but when talk show host Jessamine's Cray's stalker begins to use her past to terrorize her, no one is safe…not her family, her friends, her coworkers, and especially not Jess herself.*

## RENEGADE
### by Donna Boyd

*Enter a world of dark mystery and intense passion, where human destiny is controlled by a species of powerful, exotic creatures. Once they ruled the Tundra, now they rule Wall Street. Once they fought with teeth and claws, now they fight with wealth and power. And only one man can stop them…if he dares.*

# ALSO BY DONNA BALL

## THE LADYBUG FARM SERIES

**For every woman who ever had a dream…or a friend**

*A Year on Ladybug Farm*
*At Home on Ladybug Farm*
*Love Letters from Ladybug Farm*
*Christmas on Ladybug Farm*
*Recipes from Ladybug Farm*
*Vintage Ladybug Farm*
*The Hummingbird House*

# ABOUT THE AUTHOR

Donna Ball is the author of over a hundred novels under several different pseudonyms in a variety of genres that include romance, mystery, suspense, paranormal, western adventure, historical and women's fiction. Recent popular series include the Ladybug Farm series by Berkley Books and the Raine Stockton Dog Mystery series. Donna is an avid dog lover and her dogs have won numerous titles for agility, obedience and canine musical freestyle. She lives in a restored Victorian Barn in the heart of the Blue Ridge mountains with a variety of four-footed companions. You can contact her at http://www.donnaball.net.

26141124R00177

Made in the USA
San Bernardino, CA
20 November 2015